I0713736

RESURRECTION SAM

A Weird Western Collection

Mark Masztal

MARK MASZTAL

Published by
Not Dog Books
Office of Publication:
256 Gillette Avenue, Springfield, MA 01118 USA

First Edition: December 2022
ISBN 978-1-7330144-5-8

RESURRECTION SAM

I'd like to thank Michael Dobbs, and Karen St. Onge
for their editorial guidance and friendship.

Many thanks to Joe R. Lansdale, Brian Keene, Manly Wade Wellman,
Alan Dean Foster, Craig Johnson, Graham Masteron and John Lind
for stirring my imagination.

Special thanks to Steven Murphy for kicking my ass, showing me some
tough love, and proving to me, one word is better than two.

To my wife Kathy.
She has the eye of an eagle, the strength of a bear
and the heart of a lioness.

MARK MASZTAL

Other books by Mark Masztal:

The Chronicles of Shar-Pei

Blood In The Water

"That was the trouble with explaining with words. If you explained with gunpowder, people listened."

-Dean F. Wilson
Children of Telm, & Coilhunter Chronicles

"Western movies always seemed to show Indian women washing clothes at the creek and men with a tomahawk or spear in their hands, adorned with lots of feathers. That image has stayed in some people's minds. Many think we're either visionaries, 'noble savages,' squaw drudges or tragic alcoholics. We're very rarely depicted as real people who have greater tenacity in terms of trying to hang on to our culture and values system than most people."

-Wilma Mankiller
Native American activist and first woman elected to serve as
Principal Chief of the Cherokee Nation

"I'm your Huckleberry."

-Val Kilmer
as Doc Holliday in Tombstone

"At the resurrection, there will be the return of spirits to their bodies, the revivification of the bodies, and the remaking of the bodies."

-Said Nursi
Risale-i Nur Collection

MARK MASZTAL

Contents

··········Extras··········

Illustrations

Introduction

Resurrection Sam was born in the back dining room of Packards Restaurant in Northampton, Massachusetts.

At the time I was working as a freelance illustrator with a handful of clients. I was also illustrating a comic book mini-series, so my days were full. I had finished teaching a course in comic book art at a Boston college when the opportunity to teach a similar course at the Words & Pictures Museum in Northampton, MA became available.

For those that don't know, Kevin Eastman, co-creator of the Teenage Mutant Ninja Turtles, had bought a beautiful building on Main St. in downtown Northampton. He renovated all five floors and turned it into a wonderful place for fans to come and see some of the best comic book art in the world. It was there that I met Resurrections Sam's other father.

John Lind was working at the museum organizing events and doing graphic design work. He too was a fan of comic book art and had inked my pencils for the cover of Dogs -O-War, #3. I don't recall exactly how Sam came about, but John and I were at Packards having dinner when we started talking about a cowboy who had been hung and then resurrected. Our talks also included the crucifix scar and the zombie cowboy with the bandage over his nose.

We bounced ideas around and did some sketches. I roughed out a cover and I eventually thumbnailed the first few pages of a comic, but Sam decided he needed time to stew. Months, then years passed.

Jump ahead some twenty years when I saw there was an Australian publisher that was taking submissions for a "weird western" anthology. I decided Sam would be perfect for it, so I wrote up the story and had my trusted beta readers take a look at it to see whether or not it was a steaming pile of shit.

Sam did not make it into the anthology, but I felt that he deserved his own book, and here it is.

–Mark Masztal
Somewhere in Western Massachusetts

MARK MASZTAL

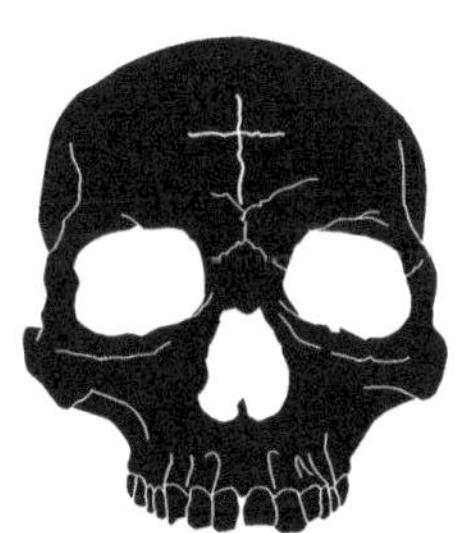

Run Sam. Run

Godammit! That bloody posse is catching up.

Sam looked back over his shoulder and saw the posse was indeed closer than they were before. They had been after him for two days now. No matter what he did, he couldn't lose them.

It wasn't his fault. That damn shit heel pressed him at the saloon and kept asking him who he was and what he was doing there. Shit, it was the Pretty Kitty. Every cowboy, rancher, blacksmith or man walking and breathing with a dick between his legs knew what you were looking for when you went to the Kitty.

It was known as the best brothel in Kansas and any man, or woman, could find anything they wanted there. Tall and short, slender and fat, white, red, brown, black or yellow-skinned. Women could find themselves a pretty boy, or a well-hung ranch hand that needed some extra coin. Giant black muscle men were always in demand. Occasionally a good-looking dandy could romance his way into their hearts and loosen their purse strings. If you wanted something a little bit different, there was a bearded lady, a pair of fat women if you wanted to be smothered. There were a few leather-ladies that would beat you until you cried for your momma.

If you were a customer who wanted to ride on the wild side, then the Pretty Kitty had a special bunkhouse set aside for that. The dead had been crawling out of their graves for years. Once in a while a posse would go out to clean up the larger groups, making sure they didn't wander close to town. If they found a dead women who wasn't too bad off, they would bring her back to the Kitty and set her up in the bunkhouse. They'd pull out all her teeth, cut off her hands and feet so the discerning customer wouldn't find himself scratched. No raging fever three days later, then croak and start his own dead shuffle. Many a customer would pay their money, go for some cold love and then chicken out once they got close to the dead woman.

Kitty management did their best to make her look as desirable as possible. Make-up, lipstick, powder and perfume usually did the trick, as would some lacey pretties. She was generally restrained at the waist on a bed or parlor couch so she wouldn't crawl away. A decent dead woman could be kept busy for months, but eventually they'd start to stink, rot and lose parts of themselves.

For customers who wanted something even wilder, there were a few mountain women that had been captured, shaved down and made to act civilized. They were close to being human, but still had a bit of animal in them when things got intense. One customer was looking to have his way with a sand devil. Management told him there was no way to secure his safety. He said he'd heard about a devil that had been trained to take on men and he wanted to try. Kitty management sent him on his way. There was no way to have sex with a devil unless you wanted to get nasty with their shit hole.

Sam kept his hat low and his bandana up to his chin. He wanted to be left alone. He was looking to get a load on and find a young painted cat to have some fun with. Not have this arsehole get in his face and press him for his name.

The man was big and fat, with long greasy black hair and a thin, droopy moustache. His hat was smashed down on his head, making his ears point in different directions and his nasty hair fan out like a lion's mane.

"I'm talking to you, boy."

"Good for you. I'm not listening."

"Who do you think you are, boy?"

"I'm someone minding his own business, just looking to get some pussy. I'm not looking for trouble."

"I think you being here is trouble. We don't want you here in town."

"You don't know me fella, so just go away." Sam turned back to the bar to enjoy his beer when the larger man put his hand on Sam's shoulder, spun him back around and stepped forward.

Bloody arsehole is big, Sam thought.

He cocked his head back and looked up at the man. He kept telling himself to keep his anger in check and not make any trouble. He wanted to do two things that night and neither was get into a fight. He worked very hard at staying out of scuffles, and now this blowhard was trying to stir up some shit.

"Listen," Sam said, "let me buy you a drink and we can go our separate ways."

"I don't want anything you got. I just want to see you gone, boy."

This fucknugget was asking for it and Sam was having a hard time keeping his temper in check. Sweat began to trickle down his neck and into his shirt.

"Did you hear me, boy? I want you to scoot!" The large man swept his hand up and knocked Sam's head back. His hat flew off into the growing crowd. Sam stepped back and doubled over, putting his face in his hands.

Bloody hell, can't walk away from this now.

Sam swung around and faced the man. Blood was trickling from his nose and his sweaty blonde hair had been swept away from his forehead. Sam's sky-blue eyes peered into the brown ones of the jackass. People always said he had spooky eyes, but now, no one was looking at his eyes. They were all focused on his scar. The rough lines of a cross had been carved on his forehead and healed white against his suntanned skin.

To add more drama, Sam pulled his bandana away from his throat, revealing the scar around his neck from a hangman's noose. The blowhard looked down at the scar and his eyes became like saucers. Originally the larger man wasn't sure whom he was giving a rash of shit to, but now he realized he had made a major mistake.

"Now you know who I am?"

"Ya – ya – yur... Resurrection Sam," whispered the large man.

"That's right. Know what it means?"

"Th-they... sez you can't die."

"Oh, I can die... you just don't want to be around when I get back up."

"Then die, ya piece of shit!" The large man looked over his shoulder to see who spoke as the gun blast ripped through the room. Sam was knocked back, landing on his backside on the dusty, sawdust-covered floor. A hole in his chest wept his life's blood across his body and onto the hungry wood. He gurgled up blood from his mouth as he struggled to catch his breath. Sweat popped out on his forehead and ran along the scar. His limbs began to seize and when they stopped dancing, his dead eyes stared up at the wood beam ceiling of the Pretty Kitty saloon.

The large man turned to see the smoking barrel of the pistol not two feet from his shoulder. He wrung his ear with his finger, trying to get the hearing back in it.

"What the hell you doing, O'Doole?"

"Look, Stanton, you weren't gonna shoot him, so I did. See, he's deader than a dried-up cow chip."

"You areshole, O'Doole. Gonna be deaf for a week."

O'Doole cracked a big shit-eating grin and patted Stanton's cheek.

"Poor corn-cracker, let me buy you a rye and make it up to ya."

"Oh... alright, ya piece of shit."

O'Doole turned to the crowd. "Where's that goddamn photographer?"

"Here, sir," came a voice from the back of the room.

"Get yer arse over here. I gotta get a picture of this."

O'Doole went to Sam's body, grabbed his feet and dragged him to the end of the bar. A smear of blood left a path the along the floor.

The photographer had his Palmer and Longking camera in place and set the three legs of the tripod. He took in the room and decided to load up his flash powder tray.

"Hurry up, fucker!" Yelled O'Doole.

"Be right there, sir."

Once set, the photographer announced that he was ready. O'Doole looked to the rest of the jackeroos around him, grabbed a beer from the bar and put a mud-caked boot on Sam's chest like a big game hunter. He cracked a shit-eating grin and stuck his chin out.

"I'm ready."

The photographer raised his flash tray, and began to count.

"On one, two."

Sam raised his head from the floor and looked up at O'Doole, "Hey fucknugget, I said you wouldn't like me when I got back up."

"Three."

O'Doole looked down as the flash tray exploded its powder and as Sam pulled the trigger of his LeMat pistol. He caught O'Doole square in the face and sprayed the back of his head onto the ceiling. The blast of the nine-shot black-powder pistol blew the body up and away from Sam, giving him the chance to roll away and get to his feet.

Half of the bar crowd was shocked by the faceless dead man lying on the floor, while the other half were astounded by the young man who had risen from the dead.

"Fuck you, Stanton," said Sam as he pistol-whipped the larger man across the face with his gun, spraying blood, spit and teeth into the faces of the cowboys behind him. The larger man dropped to the floor, moaning and gurgling in pain.

"Ya know," Sam said to the crowd, "All I wanted was to get laid. But you arseholes had to ruin it for me. Now ya'll stay where you are and I'll be leaving."

The crowd started to rumble and get ugly. Sam decided running was better than fighting. As he turned to go, he saw the photographer standing there with his mouth hanging open.

Sam cracked a smile and said, "I'll take a coupla' them prints."

He ran out of the Pretty Kitty and headed for his horse that he'd left tied down the street. Deciding that he didn't have time to get to the stables for his pack horse, he bolted out of town riding hard, hoping he could find a place to hide out and see if the shit heads in town were organized enough to pull a posse together.

Well, they were. Sam was pissed at himself. He still felt it wasn't his fault. He got ambushed, ended up dead and the fucker dared to put his foot on Sam's chest.

Sam saw the dust clouds the posse created as he rode into a small box canyon. Lucky for him, at the far end was a deserted copper mine. He tied up his horse inside and grabbed some dry brush, wiping away any tracks. He hunkered down inside the mine and hoped that the posse would lose his trail and ride by the canyon.

The horse nosed the sleeping Sam awake. He looked up, startled by the unfamiliar surroundings. He shook his head to clear it, then reached up and stroked the mare's nose.

"Hi Sweetie, you okay?"

The horse neighed and shook her head, the tips of her mane tickling his face.

Sam gave himself the moment to smile and take in the love he felt for this beautiful animal.

He then looked down at his chest and saw the tattered and stained hole in his shirt. He unbuttoned it and examined the new, puckered scar on his chest. Another one for his collection.

Sam figured he'd been asleep for a few hours. He would take a chance and look outside for the posse. He left Sweetie in the cave and ventured outside, hugging the canyon's walls and keeping an eye along the rim. He had drawn his LeMat, after replacing the spent ball, wadding and powder.

The wind had picked up and sand was blowing in the air, so he drew up his bandana over his nose. Seeing how he'd left his hat in the bar, he'd have to buy a new one. The wind whipped his long, dirty hair around his face, stinging his cheeks. He'd worn his hat so long it felt nice not wearing it.

He stepped out of the protection of the canyon walls and saw that the wind and sand had reduced visibility quite a bit. He squinted his eyes, looking for any moving shapes. He heard the distinct sound of a pistol's hammer being cocked from behind him.

"Don't move shit heel or we'll see how dead you stay with no head."

Another voice to his left said, "Drop the cannon and put your hands on your head."

Sam didn't know how many of the posse was out there, nor could he run blindly out into the sandstorm.

"Take it easy fellas, I'm putting down the iron." He slowly squatted and put the gun down in the sand. He then rose with his hands on his head. He hoped neither man could see any better than he could. He snaked his fingers down into the collar of his leather vest, searching for the throwing knife he kept there.

"So, it's really true," said a voice from in front of him. A large shape moved in from the storm and came into view. Stanton was there, holding a shotgun in his hands, with a large bandage over the left side of his face.

"You really can't die, can you?"

"Not so far. How's the face?"

"Like you care, shithead."

Sam looked around. "How many of you stuck around to wait me out?"

"Enough. Almost lost your trail except we got us a redskin tracker and he found the tracks you tried to cover up. Lucky for us because we wouldn't have seen them."

"Where's this tracker? I'd like to shake his hand. I take great pride in hiding my tracks."

The man behind him said, "No can do. We kil't him when he found yer trail. Nones of us had the coin to pay him."

This pissed Sam off. A man was killed in his name, just because he was too good of a tracker and these cheap shits were broke.

"So what do we do now?" Asked Sam.

Stanton stepped closer. "We wait for the rest of our group to find their way back. Then we're going to tie you to a horse and drag you back to town."

The voice to his left said, "We figure there won't be much left of ya after we drag you through some rocks and brush."

"I hate to spoil your sadistic dream, but someone beat ya to it, and I'm still standing."

"Speaking of standing," Stanton stepped closer, swung his shotgun and knocked Sam down on his ass.

Pain screamed through Sam's head. He saw stars and tried to catch his breath. As he lay on the ground, he felt a trembling in the sand. It was growing stronger, and in this part of the deep desert, that meant only one thing: a sand devil. He looked around for some rocky terrain and saw some, six feet behind him. He didn't know how close the devil was, but he didn't want to chance it.

He heard a couple of horses come closer and voices call out.

Stanton answered. "Over here, near the canyon opening. Follow my shot."

He aimed his shotgun into the air and pulled the trigger. The blast was deadened by the blowing wind, but it would be enough.

"Keep making noise, you arses," Sam said to himself.

The tremors continued to grow. It was just a matter of time before things got exciting.

The dead man stood on the lip of the small canyon and watched the posse surround Sam Hawkins. He held his Sharps rifle low. He didn't have a target yet and needed to see how things played out. At this distance, and with his rifle's .45-70 ammunition, he could take down any threat he saw. The wind and sand would not distract him. He actually liked how the wind felt blowing through the holes in his decomposing body. His poncho blew in the wind revealing the remains of a Confederate uniform. He had his wide brimmed Stetson pulled down low on his forehead. His cast-over white eyes sat deep in their sockets and his dark, receding gums gave him a death grin that frightened everyone who saw it. Blood, puss and snot stained the swath of bandage covering the hole where his nose used to be. It kept the sand out of his sinuses and for that he was glad.

"How long... has it been, Sam? –"

"How long ago... did I carve that... cross... into your skin? –"

"How... long ago did you... shoot me in the face... and kill me? –"

"How long must I... chase you until we are both... dead?"

He heard a croaking whinny behind him and glanced back at his undead horse. One side of its face had been stripped to the bone and some of its ribs were starting to break through its tightening skin. The dead man turned back to the conflict below as the sandstorm ramped up.

As Sam lay on the sandy ground, he watched as more men emerged from the sandstorm. He now counted six including Stanton and the first two he encountered. The idiots were stomping around and firing their weapons. You would think experienced cowboys in this part of the state would know not to make a lot of noise in the desert. He had a feeling they did some drinking before setting out after him.

"You boys took your sweet time finding us," said Stanton. Two of the men came out of the sandstorm.

"It's not like you made it easy, Stanton," said Rodgers.

"We've been wandering around bumping into boulders and brush," said Bourgeot.

"I don't give a rat's ass if you were bumping each other's butt cheeks. When I say jump, I want you here," said Stanton.

Rodgers and Bourgeot looked at each other with scowls on their faces. They didn't need this shit. They'd been happy drinking at the Pretty Kitty, but Stanton was their ranch boss and he demanded obedience.

"All you yahoos keep an eye on this jerk-weed, until the rest of the boys show up. We'll drag his sorry ass back to town and then make sure he stays dead."

Sam didn't like the sound of that. He took note of where the men were and started to slowly edge toward the stone ledges behind him.

The sound of horses approaching made the group turn to see who was arriving.

"Who goes there?" Shouted Stanton.

"Charlie Evans and Calvin Tabb."

"Get your asses over here, we got business to do."

A loud hissing noise broke through the sound of the wind. The men all looked around with questioning looks on their faces.

"You hear that?"

"What the fuck *is* that?"

"I don't like this, Stanton."

"Shut the fuck up, you pansies. Keep your eyes open."

The hissing noise grew louder. Sam had finally made it to the stone ledge while the posse got distracted. He hurried to the safety of some large boulders and hunkered down.

Evans and Tabb emerged from the storm just as there was an explosive eruption of sand and dirt. Evans and his horse rocketed into the sky. As the sand cleared, a huge sand devil came into view, carrying the man and horse, trapped in its mandibles. Its reddish mahogany body was segmented, and it had a large, copper-colored shell covering its head. Sprouting from the back of its head were the pair of fleshy horns that gave the beast its name. The creature's mandibles were massive and chomping wildly at its prey. Man and horse were being torn to pieces as arms, feet, hooves, haunches and organs spilled to the sand. The devil reached its apex, waved its six spiny legs into the air, then dove back down after Tabb and the other men.

"Holy shit!"

"Fuckin' sand devil!"

"No shit!"

The screams of the dying men tore through the sound of the storm, while those still alive drew their weapons and began shooting at the beast. Bullets sank into its mucous-covered red hide. Others ricocheted off its armored head. The beast reared up and brought all its weight down on Tabb and his horse. The horse's innards burst from its stomach, spraying the men with blood, bile and gore. Tabb wasn't so lucky. Pinned under his horse, he was pressed flat into the soft sand, his chest, spine and skull crushed like eggshell.

Sam looked over the boulder and watched the ravaging of the men and horses. He had felt the vibrations of the approaching sand devil, and knew to hide. He'd tangled with them in the past, and barely survived. He was just fine sitting behind the boulder, watching the show.

The shooting continued but there was much less of it. He could see a few man shapes moving in the storm and a much larger one moving too quickly for something so big.

Eventually the shooting stopped, and Sam stood to see if anyone was left alive. He saw a man stumbling toward the stone shelf, collapsing once he was on solid ground. Sam came from around the boulder and walked up to the prone man. He went to pull his pistol, but realized it was still lying in the sand, twenty feet away. Instead, he slid his bowie knife from its hip scabbard and crept forward. The man began to stir and then suddenly bolted upright, pistol pointed at Sam.

"Did you think it would be that easy, Sam?"

"I kinda did, Stanton. You have fun dancing with the devil?"

"Goddamn you, boy! All my men are dead and here you are standing safe and sound."

"Could be that's because I've dealt with the devils before and know they can't move through rock."

"I'll give you that, but because of you, there are a lot of good men dead."

"'Good men?' One of your 'good men' shot me dead. And then when that didn't work, the rest of ya was looking to lynch me."

"You goddamn deserved it, ya freak-a-nature."

"So what do we do now, Stanton? You're in no shape to be walking back to town and we both know ya can't kill me."

The bigger man tried to stand up straight and found he couldn't. He coughed up blood and grabbed at his ribs. Probably broke when that damn sand devil swept past him and sent him ass over teakettle.

Damn freaky kid was right, now what do I do?

"I don't care if I can't kill ya. Maybe I'll just keep shootin' you every time you sit up. Maybe when you're dead I feed you to that damn devil? What do you think of that, shit-heel?" Said Stanton as he aimed his pistol at Sam's face.

Sam didn't know where the shot came from – the canyon played tricks with sound – but he heard it clear as a bell over the storm. He recognized it as the crack of a Sharps rifle. Stanton's upper face and head exploded in a burst of brains, gore and bits of skull. From the neck up, only his ears, lower jaw and droopy moustache remained. The pistol fell from his hand, bouncing on the shale ledge. His knees buckled and his body toppled over into a heap upon the rocks.

Sam spun around, looking all around for the shooter, finally spying him standing upon the canyon's ridge.

"Hello there, Lieutenant Mace," he said under his breath, and nodded his head. Sam stood as straight as could be knowing a rifle was pointed at him. After waiting a couple seconds and not eating a bullet, he grabbed his pistol and beat feet for the mine.

He got on Sweetie's back and rode as hard as he could away from that box canyon, always expecting to get one in the back. He'd sneak into town when it got dark. He'd get his packhorse and supplies, and ride as far away from this territory as luck would take him. Sam hoped the dead man didn't get that close again for a very long time.

The thing that had been Lieutenant Mace stood and watched as Resurrection Sam rode away into the sand storm and back towards town. He'd eventually have his chance, but for now, this wasn't the time or place for ending it all. He turned back to his undead horse, put his rifle in its scabbard and pulled himself up into the saddle. The horse made a noise like dry branches being twisted. The dead man looked back at the boy riding away.

"Run, Sam. Run."

I guess this story is a world-building ten pounds of shit, in a five pound bag.

I throw the reader into the middle of a chase, and then backtrack to explain why our young, bad-mouthed gunslinger is running for his life. All he wanted was to get drunk and laid, preferably in that order. What he got instead was shot and pissed off.

This story was influenced by Joss Whedon's Firefly (2002), Norman Macdonnel and John Meston's Gunsmoke (1955 - 1975), and I tried to achieve the attitude of George P. Cosmatos and Kevin Jarre's Tombstone (1993).

I found Sam's, LeMat black-powder pistol in a search for mid-1880's western weapons, along with Mace's Sharp's rifle. Both were slow to reload, but the cool factor with the LeMat is it has nine chambers for firing a decent grain shot, as well as a lower chamber for shooting birdshot like a shotgun. The LeMat served its owner well and makes many appearances throughout this collection.

As for the sand devil, it was an interesting name that jumped into my head. From there I tried my best to have it influenced more by worms and grubs, than by Dune or Beetlejuice.

The Hanged Man's Tale

The recently hung body swayed back and forth from the old, skeletal tree. The other hanged man sat on his horse and gazed up at the dead body. He silently thanked whatever force of nature brought him back from the dead. He also cursed that same force of nature for condemning him to a life of death, resurrection, death and more resurrection.

As he pushed back his beat-up Stetson, revealing strands of sweaty blond hair and a cross-shaped scar on his forehead, Resurrection Sam took in the horrors the body had suffered. Crows had plucked out its eyes like large, delicious grapes, while other birds and creatures had mounted the corpse's face and dined on its nose, ears and lips.

Something else had delved deep into the man's torso and removed the liver and sweet kidneys. The intestines hung in a looping mess down to the sandy, dry ground. He didn't know of any natural animal that could get up that high and leave that amount of damage.

Sam dismounted his horse and cuddled her long fawn head.

"What do you think, Sweetie? A zombie? A vamp? *Hestovatohkeo'o* is possible, but they like their victims breathin' and we're too far south for *Mishipeshu*." From behind Sam his packhorse whinnied.

"Hello Larry, feeling left out?"

The horse flipped his head up and shook it.

"You're the hardest working horse in the territories, aren't you?"

The dark brown Morgan blew air out of his nostrils and flapped his lips.

"Aren't you so silly."

Sam gave Larry a quick kiss on his snout and turned and walked towards the body, avoiding the entrails as much as he could. The open wound looked torn, not cut, and he saw bite marks on some of the bones. He walked around the body and saw at least six different boot marks ... and two sets of bare feet.

"What the fuck?"

Sam stepped back and looked around the area. He saw four structures at four different locations, but couldn't identify them. He walked back to Sweetie and drew out a set of beat-up military binoculars from his saddlebag. He focused on the structures and realized they were cemetery gates. He removed his compass out of a coat pocket and took readings of the four sites.

Who the hell would build four cemeteries at the four points of the compass around a hanging tree? He thought to himself.

He turned around in dismay, trying to figure the situation out. He went back to the footprints. Sam saw both pairs headed north, so he followed them up to the gate of the north cemetery, which was surrounded by a low wrought iron fence. All the headstones were very old. Some were so old that their engravings had been worn away by the wind and sand. Dry grass had sprung up all around. He saw Catholic, Methodist, Presbyterian, and Millerite headstones next to older markers that looked like Pagan, Wiccan, and Northern European. His eyes followed the footprints to a large dirt mound in the center of the cemetery. There, a small metal gate was set into the side of the mound. There were symbols scratched into the stones surrounding the gate. Sam knew what this all meant.

"Goddamn ghouls."

Sam hadn't seen a ghoul since he was in Pennsylvania, some years ago. They creeped him out. Not only did they try to eat you; they were always women and would sweet-talk you.

Sam backtracked and ran to the other three cemeteries. He saw old and new footprints coming and going to the hanging tree.

"Sons of bitches."

He didn't know how close the nearest town was, but he could tell no one had been buried in these cemeteries in a long time. The townsfolk had been bringing dead offerings to these fetid creatures. They probably thought it would keep them from going into town and having a light snack. He also didn't believe any town around these parts would have enough natural deaths to satiate four groups of ghouls.

Judging from his hung friend, they'd been making full-blown sacrifices. Fucking weird trouble always seemed to find him. Was there no place in the territories that offered some peace and quiet?

This shitty situation needed fixing, and he guessed it was up to him. It was time to take account of his supplies and make a plan.

Sam took the horses half a mile away for their safety. He'd gone through his saddlebags and pulled out the items he thought he would need. He made sure he had full loads in his LeMat, black powder 9-shot pistol. His plan was to wait until dark and see what showed up and then deal with them righteously.

Bare feet shuffled through the tall grass, stirring up the dry topsoil, causing dust to billow into the air. The first pair of feet was joined by a second as they travelled down the small hill towards the hanging tree. The ghouls had left good bits behind the night before and it was time to relish them after their aging in the daytime sun. As they got closer to the tree, they saw a campfire burning, but there were no signs of men. Their eyes were sharper in the dark, but these two ghouls were hundreds of years old: time diminishes one's senses, even for undead ghouls. They both looked at each other in curiosity. No one living ever stayed here after the sun set. They sniffed the air, but the wood smoke masked hundreds of odors flitting through the light breeze.

"Sister... what is it?"

"I don't know... sister," answered the second ghoul.

"I... don't see... or smell... anything."

"I... am hungry, sister."

"Yes... "

The two ghouls picked up their pace as they got closer to the hanging tree. They were of average height, but terribly thin, almost to the point of skeletal. Their skin was a sickly grey and smeared with dirt, dried blood and unspeakable fluids. They wore torn and dirty shifts that barely covered their nudity. It was the only thing that reminded them of when they were different, when they were warm, when they were human. Their unwashed and snarled hair fell half way down their backs, littered with twigs, leaves, bits of grass and dried blood.

Their eyes were sunken in their sockets, the corneas a washed-out grey. Living underground and only coming out at night had given them the gift of night vision, but any type of bright light blinded them, causing excruciating pain.

The sisters ate flesh and organs, so their teeth were made for biting and tearing. Crooked, over-sized, and sharp as daggers, their yellow teeth were their main weapons, but their ragged nails came into use, too.

They came to the hanged man and danced and gyrated below him, like he was still alive and could appreciate the suggestive movements. One of the sisters looked up at the open torso, licked her lips with a disgusting black and purple tongue, and leapt up to the corpse. Her nails sank into the decomposing flesh as she wrapped her legs around the body like a long forgotten lover, anchoring herself with her feet. She reached into the body cavity, plucked out a nasty morsel and plopped it into her mouth. She leaned back with a hideous smile and chewed her treat.

"It's so good... sister."

"Save some for me." The other ghoul darted into the dark and scrambled up the tree.

The first ghoul had her face buried in the corpse's body cavity and was shaking her head from side-to-side, tearing at the remaining organs. She leaned back out of the body, her face a mask of blood and gore. She looked up to the sky with a hideous grin on her face, as her hands caressed her skeletal body. Her breasts were almost non-existent, but she took pleasure in touching herself. This was the happiest she had ever been.

"Hey fuckface," Sam said to her while clinging to the tree branch above the hung body. "Sam says smile." He aimed his LeMat pistol, cocked the striker, flicked its top lever forward and pulled the trigger, firing through the shotgun barrel. He gave the ghoul a face full of #4 buckshot. It tore through her face, pulping her nose and exploding her eyes like two rotten eggs. Most of the shot passed through her head, but some of the deadly pellets ricocheted inside her skull. They liquefied what was left of the ghoul's rotted brain.

The dead body sagged and let go of its grasp on the hanging corpse. It fell to the dusty ground and lay still. Blood soaked the sandy ground below it.

"Sister!" A shout from above.

Sam jerked his head around and saw the other ghoul stepping onto the branch that he was wrapped around.

"What did you do?" The ghoul screamed.

"Oh shit," he whispered to himself.

The ghoul dropped to all fours and began stalking him like a mountain lion. She ranted about her sister and what she was going to do to him, and what part of him she would chew on first. Sam didn't like the sound of that, so he took in his situation and decided a dumb move was the best. He shimmied closer to the end of the branch but, unluckily for him, it started to dip and sway. The branch could handle the weight of a dead man, but add on a live body plus a ghoul, and it started to bend. As it did, Sam lost his balance and toppled downward, losing both grip and pistol. As he began to fall, he desperately reached out and hugged his dead friend. He slid down the corpse until his hand slipped inside its torso, landing atop the corpse's pelvic bone. He grabbed on tight like his life depended on it... which it did.

He might survive the fall, but a broken leg or back would leave him prime ghoul entrée.

He swayed back and forth and apologized to his dead friend about the death-grip he had on his private area, when he heard a cackle from above him.

The ghoul realized Sam's situation and came down the rope until she was crouched on the dead man's shoulders with her putrid cooze on top of his head.

"Look what's… happened… to you."

"This?" Sam said, smiling. "It's part of my master plan."

"It's a… stupid plan."

Yes it is, he thought to himself.

His mind was racing, trying to find an answer to his situation. There was only one thing to do. He reached across his body and drew the large bowie knife from its scabbard on his thigh. The ghoul came at him, hanging upside down like a spider. She was so close he could smell her awful breath; a mix of soil, old blood and spoiled meat.

She came at him mouth first, which worked for him. As the ghoul came closer, he swung his arm up, driving his knife towards her head.

Two things happened that worked in his favor. One was his knife rammed into the ghoul's skull. The creature froze as the electric synapses that fired its muscles suddenly stopped. Second, the frayed rope that hung Sam's dead friend snapped. All three bodies fell to the ground.

The ghoul landed on its face and didn't move. Sam landed on his back with his new best friend landing on top of him. His hand erupted out of its back as its body's weight finally accepted Sir Isaac's theory of gravity.

Sam lay on the ground for a few seconds before he tensed, preparing for another attack, when he realized that both ghouls were dead. They all lay on the ground like lovers staring up at a romantic, starry night.

He rolled his friend off him, extracted his hand from the body and shook any gore onto the ground. Sam found his pistol in the dirt, then went over to the ghoul he had stabbed in the head and retrieved his knife. He dragged her over to the campfire and tossed her onto the flames. The ghoul caught fire and erupted in a burst of blue flame. Sam stumbled back as the heat drove him away from the fire.

He went to the ghoul he shot in the face, grabbed her by the hair, he hefted her up and helped her join her sister in the fire. Smoke billowed as the body landed and sparks exploded into the air. Sam decided he would show his hanged friend the respect he deserved by burying him away from the fire.

As the fire started to die down, the sisters looked like so much burnt kindling, slowly turning to ash. For Sam, step one was done. Now he needed to complete his plan.

He ran over to a pile of dead branches and straw grass he had covered his saddlebag with. He slung it over his shoulder and headed up to the sisters' cemetery. He pulled out three sticks of dynamite joined by a long fuse. He lit it and lobbed the explosive through the gate that led to the ghouls' underground tomb. Sam ran to the next two cemeteries and repeated the same actions. Arriving at the last one, he lit the short fuse and reared back to throw it when he heard, "What are... you doing... little man?"

Dirty fingers wrapped around the wrought iron gate to the burial mound as a hideous face pushed itself against the bars, staring out at Sam.

"I'm about to show you that men fight back against you terrible things."

Sam tossed the lit dynamite through the gate bars, past the ghoul, and into the depths of the burial mound.

The ghoul watched the dynamite go past her face, realized what it was and scrambled down a dark corridor after it. "Nooooooooo!" Her scream diminished as she went deeper.

Sam was already running back to the tree when the first cemetery exploded with a flash of light, fire and booming thunder. As he arrived back at the tree, the other two cemeteries exploded in succession. Finally the fourth went up. All the cemeteries burned as dry grasses, twigs and branches caught fire around the headstones. Sam hoped that the explosions had killed all the ghouls while they slept, or buried them under tons of rock and dirt.

Sam dropped to his knees. Running from site to site and everything that had happened up in the tree had taken its toll on him. He couldn't die, but he physically had his limits and he just met them. He closed his eyes, took a deep breath and passed out.

By the time Resurrection Sam woke up, the sun had risen, the cemeteries had burned themselves out and smoke drifted away in the breeze. He had no interest in checking each cemetery to see if all the ghouls were dead. Instead he went and buried the hanged man, saying some kind words over his grave. He then gathered his horses and rode to the campfire.

He stirred up the coals with a branch until a spark caught it aflame. He went to the hanging tree, jammed the flaming branch into a deep crevice and set it on fire. The hanging tree blazed brighter than the rising sun. The resurrected man rode away.

There would be no more hangings here.

I knew that for the second Resurrection Sam story, I wanted to focus on Sam and his horses, but I also wanted to have two contrasting hanged men in the story. For this I turned to two of the storytellers that have inspired me, Mike Mignola and Brian Keene.

Mike Mignola's The Ghoul (2005), gave us a well-dressed ghoul just looking for a quick bite. Of course, paranormal detective and member of the Burreau for Paranormal Research and Defense, Hellboy, showed the ghoul a thing or two.

Brian Keene's novel, Ghoul (2007), gave us three childhood friends living in a small town who discover a ghoul has taken up residence under the local graveyard. It threatens their small town, and their friends, so they deal with it as best they can, but with heavy losses. A side story involved child abuse that some say was the true evil of the story.

I had to involve a couple of ghouls and to my surprise folklore said that they are always women, so I created the sisters. Ghouls are nasty, smelly corpse-eating creatures, but I also wanted to express the feminity of the ghouls. I also needed to bring the gross factor up a couple notches and of course that meant using the dearly departed and his internal organs.

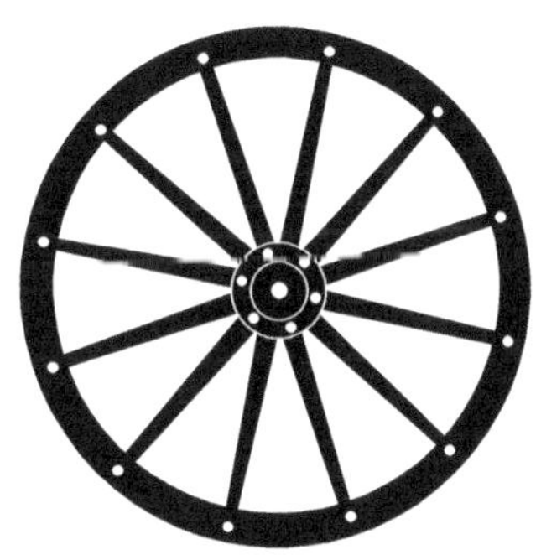

Bloodcoach

It was supposed to be a simple job.

Two Trees Holmes and Resurrection Sam Hawkins had met at the Pretty Kitty, where Two Trees worked as a stud to those women who could afford it. He also hired out to do odd jobs to make spare cash. He wanted to pay off his contract with the management of the saloon and end his servitude with them. It was friends like Sam that often brought him high paying jobs that helped him build his bankroll.

Two Trees was half African and half Shawnee Nation, and he got the best of both races. He stood seven feet tall, had dark burgundy skin, straight, shiny black hair and a muscular build that made him the desire of most women, and some men.

He was named Two Trees because of the size of his thighs when he was a baby. As a man, some people had another name for him, Three Trees. It was rumored that the giant had a cock the length of a normal man's thigh. This was something Sam had no interest in verifying. He just enjoyed the giant's quiet nature. Plus, they worked well together when hired out.

Sam and Two Trees were approached to drive a stagecoach loaded with supplies, medicine, a local doctor and his nurse, from Wichita,

Kansas to Red River Valley, Texas. It was a three hundred and fifty-mile trip that contained some well cut trails, but for the most part the stagecoach would be blazing new trails through the wilderness. The two men guessed it would be a six-day, round-trip adventure, that paid three hundred dollars apiece, including supplies. That three hundred would make a huge dent in Two Trees' war chest. Any money more than five dollars would help Sam on his constant nomadic trip to stay alive and ahead of the dead man who hunted him, Lieutenant Ambrose Mace.

The men looked at each other over the bar room table and thought about the deal. They'd be leaving in two days if they took the job. Sam knew what the money meant to his friend, and he wanted him out of the Pretty Kitty. He was afraid that as the giant man got older, his attraction would wane, and he'd become more of a curiosity than he already was. His ranking among the other male escorts would fall and he'd be delegated to the more sordid of trysts, eventually released from his contract for lack of profit-making. That usually meant being sold off as an indentured slave to a coal mine or railroad company. In his prime, Two Trees could do the work of three men, but after years of abuse and growing old, that kind of work was a death sentence.

Two Trees didn't know everything about Sam, but he knew why he was called 'Resurrection.' He'd seen it happen, but had no clue why Sam was always on the move.

The men reached across the table and shook the hand of the stage line representative. Each was paid one hundred dollars in advance to buy supplies. They must provide their own weapons. The plan was to meet in front of the livery stable and leave in two days. When the representative left, they ordered a round of whiskey, toasted each other, and headed out to buy supplies and prepare.

Two days later the men were in front of the Wichita Livery viewing the stagecoach they'd be driving. It looked like your regular coach, but that's where the similarities ended. This one had been reinforced with heavy planking along its sides and top. Iron bars were over the windows. It was loaded down with wooden crates at its rear and on the roof. There were four horses harnessed and pawing at the ground, itching to leave. They were strong-looking Morgans. That put a smile on Sam's face. His packhorse, Larry, was a Morgan whom he thought of as the hardest working horse in the West.

The men greeted the stagecoach representative, made small talk, and were introduced to their passengers, Doctor Davis Shane, and his nurse, Alyson Strong. Shane was a short man with glasses, greased hair parted down the middle, a small, trimmed moustache and a fancy suit and tie. Nurse Strong wore a simple ladies dress adorned with pretty flowers, and a small hat pinned to her auburn hair. She had dazzling green eyes. She caught Sam's eye right away but seemed stand-offish, only saying "hello" when introduced.

When asked what they would be carrying, Doc Shane said it was medical supplies. That was all he would say. Sam and Two Trees were hired to drive the stagecoach, and not ask questions. Just make it to Red River Valley. They made sure the stagecoach was tight and ready to travel, assisted their two passengers, and mounted the coach. Two Trees took the reins, giving them a quick shake. The Morgans pulled away from the livery stable as they headed out of town.

Fifty miles later, the drivers switched. Sam had the reins while Two Trees napped behind him among the supply boxes. The passengers were silent, so to be honest, Sam was bored as shit. A little excitement would have been welcomed. Just nothing too exciting.

Eventually, he heard a knock from behind him.

"Hello. Can you hear me?" It was Shane.

"Watcha need?"

"We need to take a break."

Two Trees sat up behind Sam. "I could piss."

"With something that big, best not flood us out." Two Trees made a sour face that Sam didn't see.

"Okay," said Sam to the passengers. "Hang tight."

He looked ahead and saw a tall tree with shade, and a small stream beyond it. It would be good to water the horses and let them nibble some grass. The stagecoach came to a halt. Sam jumped down and opened the coach door. Nurse Strong extended her hand and Sam helped her step down. Doc Shane was nimbler than he looked and hopped out on his own and headed straight for a copse of trees. It seemed like the doctor was in a bit of a hurry. Two Trees dropped down from the coach and made his own way to some trees. It looked like it was up to Sam to tend to the nurse. He drew his pistol and escorted her closer to the stream.

"I can handle this myself, Mister Hawkins."

"Ma'am, it's my job to make sure you get from Wichita to Red River Valley safely."

She made a frown and looked put out.

After a few yards, Sam said, "This is far as I go. You'll have the privacy you need and still be protected."

Sam turned his back. The nurse wandered closer to the stream until she felt comfortable enough to squat and make water. She wore simple knickers and a light petticoat. She had no need to wear a lot of layers; her goal on this long trip was to be comfortable. She had known Doc Shane for seven years and found he did not have any manly urges towards her. She was not worried about any inappropriate advances. She was still unsure about the two drivers. The giant man looked scary, but he seemed friendly enough. Sam was a little scrapper and there was something about him that made her feel like she wanted to get to know him better.

Sam was quietly daydreaming and taking in the cloudless sky when the nurse strode past him and headed to the stagecoach.

"Thank you, Mister Hawkins." She didn't make eye contact, just walked right by him. He did think he saw a small smirk on her face. Maybe his chivalry might get him somewhere.

Sam hopped onto the stagecoach and took over Two Trees' spot on the roof of the coach. Two Trees mounted the coach. "I was not finished taking my nap."

"I drew nurse duty, now I get to nap."

The large man thought this over and decided he'd give this one to the little man. He checked to make sure the passengers were back in the coach, and then got the horses moving. They travelled for four hours before pulling over to camp for the night. Doc Shane tried to argue this, but Sam and Two Trees won the argument. They were beat, road worn and hungry as bears. Nothing was going to stop them from getting some chow and shuteye.

After camp was set, it was decided that the doctor and nurse would sleep inside the coach, and Sam and Two Trees would alternate between keeping watch and sleeping under the coach. Sam got a roaring fire going and was preparing to cook dinner when he suggested that the nurse should take the cooking duties. Sam's chivalry took a mighty plunge when he found out the nurse could not cook and usually ate at the local café. She gave him a look suggesting that even though she was a woman, how dare he assume she could cook.

With dinner finished, everyone broke for the evening. Sam took the first watch by setting himself up on the roof of the coach. The horses had been watered, fed and were tied up near a copse of trees.

Sam was armed with his LeMat pistol and a '73 Winchester rifle. He also had a lantern, a blanket, a canteen full of water and a British copy of Lewis Carroll's *Alice in Wonderland*. Sam identified with Alice. He was trapped in a world that he sometimes didn't recognize. Because of a weird twist of fate, he could not escape. He was surrounded by weird and wonderful characters, and always tucked away in some dark place in his mind, was his Red Queen, Lieutenant Ambrose Mace.

The evening was quiet. Sam kept himself entertained by reading and keeping watch. He woke Two Trees at two and went to sleep under the coach.

Once the sun dawned, Two Trees got the horses harnessed and ready for the day. Sam started a fire and got coffee and johnnycakes going. Once everyone was dressed and fed, the coach pulled out for another long day.

The weather was pleasant and sunny. There was a slight breeze that made the travelling comfortable. Two Trees had passed the reins over to Sam but decided to stay up front. Sam had his hat off; the wind blowing his hair back, exposing his cross-shaped scar.

"You never told me how you got your scar."

"Never thought you cared."

"We are friends. If you asked me anything, I would tell you."

Sam thought about it for a few seconds. "I was going to be hanged for killing a man, which I felt was self-defense. The weak-willed judge was persuaded to sentence me for murder. It seems I riled up the anger of a Lieutenant Mace. He was a Confederate soldier that had found God. He felt I was too much a heathen. I reckon my mouth had gotten me into trouble, and Mace didn't take kindly to it."

"So there I was, standing center stage in front of town, hands tied behind my back with a preacher asking if I wanted my soul to be saved. Well, my mouth opened on its own and Mace didn't like what came out. He knocked me down, pulled out his knife and gave me this wonderful scar on my head." Sam pointed to his forehead.

"I guess the town was a 'scared of him, so the hangman stood me back up with blood running all down my face. He put a hood over my head, and tightened the noose around my neck. I had some choice words for the town and Mace and then the next thing I know, I'm dropping like two bags of shit and the rope made me dance in the air. I blacked out and the next thing I know I'm lying on the ground. The hood's off my face, and the crowd is running around looking like they just pissed themselves."

"How did it feel?"

"The rope?"

Two Trees nodded. He was enraptured by Sam's story.

"It felt like shit, especially the snapping part. Anyway, I'm told the doctor said I was dead, and they'd dragged me out into the sun, for everyone to see. Then, in front of the crowd, I took in a deep breath, sat up and looked around. While everyone was standing there with fear in their eyes, I grabbed a deputy's gun and got to my feet. I laughed a few times, kind of evil like, and told them to back off. They'd hung me and it didn't take, so I wasn't going to give them a second chance.

Well, old Mace comes charging at me and I shot him. Now mind you, I wasn't too steady, because you know, I'd just been hung. So instead of shooting him in the chest, I blew off his nose."

"No nose?"

"Yup, just a big bloody ragged hole. Well, this pissed him off, but by then I had run through the crowd 'n hopped on a horse and was looking to get the fuck outta town. I looked back and the Lieutenant was cursing and swearing he would catch me, all the while spraying blood and snot all over the crowd. I took aim again, and this time I didn't miss."

"Dead?"

"Kind of."

"What do you mean?"

"Lieutenant Ambrose Mace was dead, but two days later, he rose as one of the walking dead and swore vengeance on me. He's been chasing me ever since."

"But, Sam, the dead are mindless. All they do is walk around looking to eat people. How can he be chasing you?"

"I don't know, but it's like me being hung dead, and then resurrected in front of the whole town."

Sam reached up and drew away the bandana that was around his throat. Two Trees saw the rope marks around the younger man's neck.

"This is the second scar Mace gave me, and I have no intention of having him give me a third."

Nurse Strong leaned away from the inside wall of the coach after hearing Sam's brief recounting, and settled in her seat. She thought about what he said and couldn't believe most of it, but she had seen the rope marks, although not the other scar. She looked over at Doctor Shane. His feet were up, and he was napping. It seemed the motion of the stagecoach lulled him to sleep like it would a small baby. If she had a quiet moment along the way, she would press Sam Hawkins to show her his forehead.

The second day of travel ended quietly. The coach and its occupants had stopped twice for piss breaks and lunch. They finally stopped around six for dinner and a good night's sleep. Nurse Strong had helped Sam with dinner, and had smiled at him, making him blush.

Doctor Shane kept himself busy puttering around with his supplies, which he still would not discuss. Sam was hoping he could get some information from the nurse and then pass it along to Two Trees. The big black native had unharnessed the horses, watered and fed them. He tied them out near some low bushes, and they were happy nibbling leaves and swishing their tails back and forth to keep the flies away.

Sam agreed to take first watch and like the past night, got himself all set on top of the coach with Alice and her friends.

"The Queen turned crimson with fury, and, after glaring at her for a moment like a wild beast, began screaming 'Off with her head! Off with—'

"Nonsense!" Said Alice, very loudly and decidedly, and the Queen was silent. —"

Sam heard a noise, like heavy sheets caught in a windstorm, slapping against themselves. The sound grew louder, closer. Something flew by Sam, something big, fast and extremely rank. It smelled like no animal he had ever been around, like the stench of rotting flesh, and death.

Sam waited a couple seconds and then whatever it was passed by again. This time, he heard more flapping sounds in the distance, and he knew they were in trouble.

Scrambling down from the top of the coach, he slapped his hands on the door.

"Get up! Get up! We got trouble!"

He bent over and looked under the coach. "Trees! Get your ass up, we got trouble!"

A loud rumbling came from under the coach, together with the sound of a massive body moving around. Two Trees had heard Sam.

Sam ran over to the horses and untied the larger two of the four.

He got them to the harnesses and hooked up. A few more sweeping sounds followed him back to the other horses. He looked around into the night sky but didn't see anything, still, it didn't mean danger was not in the air. The younger horses were a bit skittish. They fought him the entire way to the coach, not settling down once he had them lashed into the harnesses.

Two Trees had rolled out from under the stagecoach and stood ready, armed with his Winchester rifle.

"What's going on?"

Sam looked at him. "Something's flying around and it smells like shit."

Doctor Shane opened the coach and peered out. "What's the trouble, driver?"

Sam ran over to him. "Doc, you get back in there and buckle up. Something is targeting us and we're getting the hell out of here."

"I don't see anything –" Something wide and leathery swept between the two men, knocking Sam to the ground and forcing Shane back inside.

Two Trees raised his rifle and began shooting at anything he saw moving in the sky. He had eight rounds to let loose before he had to reload. He was hoping to make each one count. Sam got back to his feet and drew his LeMat. The black powder pistol was shit for long-range accuracy, but if the target was close enough, he'd blow one hell of a hole in it.

"Reloading!" Said Two Trees.

"I got you."

Sam kept shooting his nine-shot pistol and heard at least three hit flesh. Whatever was up there could be killed, he hoped. Three-shots, two-shots and then one final shot.

"I'm out!" He yelled.

"You are covered," said Two Trees.

The big man kept firing while Sam holstered his pistol, then jumped up on the wheel of the coach and reached for his rifle. It was fully loaded so he immediately dropped down and started shooting into the air.

"Do we run out of ammo or run for the hills?" Asked Two Trees.

Sam looked around and weighed their odds. "I say we run like crazy and hope we're lucky."

"I will take the reins while you reload," said Two Trees, tossing Sam his rifle.

"Yup."

Sam ran up to the coach window and looked inside. He saw Doc Shane curled up on the floor while the nurse was kneeling on the seat, holding a pair of scalpels at the ready. It smelled like someone had pissed themselves. Probably the doctor.

"You okay?" Asked Sam.

"To be honest, I'm scared shitless," said Alyson with a quick smile.

Sam grinned at the nurse's swear. It meant she wasn't so frigid after all.

"Me too. Hang tight, we're going to run."

Sam climbed up to the roof. Two Trees shook the reins and the horses started to trot. Another quick jerk, with some verbal persuasion, and they picked up speed. The horses were scared and realized that running might keep them alive.

Sam reloaded Two Trees' enormous '76 Winchester and his smaller '73. He kept on looking around for anything trying to strafe him or the stagecoach. He saw figures and shadows out of the corner of his eye, but nothing came close enough for him to shoot. Two Trees was driving the team of horses harder than he should, but this was a desperate situation. Suddenly the air around them was alive with leathery wings, talons, fangs, and blazing red eyes. Sam began shooting both rifles. He heard a couple of screeches of pain. This gave him some satisfaction. Damned if he would become vamp food. Yup, had to be vampires out there. He hadn't seen one in a few years, and last time it was just a matter of hiding out and waiting for the sun to rise. But they were hours away from that, and these vamps were more like wild beasts than the ones he had dealt with before.

Suddenly the stagecoach was rocked by a collision. He heard a scream behind him. Sam spun to his left and saw a nightmare clinging to the side of the coach. It was the size of a man and naked, but that's where the similarities stopped. Its skin was cold grey, and looked dry. Creases were everywhere there was a joint. The thing's arms, hands and fingers were deformed into long thin limbs. Leathery skin stretched between its fingers. The wings were at least ten feet wide, and it had hooks on the ends that were anchored into the wood of the coach. Its skull had sparse hairs along the sides and it had large, leaf-shaped ears. The eyes were savage and glared red, the nose wide and leathery, its mouth open wide revealing a mouthful of needle sharp teeth.

Hearing the nurse scream, the vampire turned its attention to her. Seeing warm blood and flesh to tear, it began ripping at the wooden door. Unable to get through the iron bars over the window, it began to lock its feet onto the door, hoping to rip it off its hinges. Before it had a chance, Sam used his shotgun to blow one hooked talon off, loosening its grip on the roof. He fired Two Trees' larger gun and blew a hole in its chest. The blast went clean through its body, spraying flesh, bone and dark blood onto the ground. The beast still hung onto the coach, but it was weakening. Before Sam could fire another shot, the nurse snaked a hand between the bars and sliced into the remaining talon holding onto the roof. The creature tumbled back and fell in a heap onto the hard packed earth.

"Hot damn, nurse Strong!" Yelled Sam.

Sam cut his celebration short. Three more of the flying creatures were now tearing at the crates of medical supplies tied to the boot. They savagely went at the crates, as though searching for something special. He was about to start firing at the three when he heard, "Oh shit," from the front of the coach.

He turned and saw Two Trees looking back at him with fear in his eyes. He looked out in front of them and saw an enormous shadow coming their way. It was twice the size of the stagecoach and bigger than any of the grizzly bears he'd encountered. Its two red eyes glared at them with hate. Before they knew, it was upon them. It slammed into the horses and pushed them, and their harnesses, back into the stagecoach. Sam saw Two Trees get bowled over by one of the rear horses but before he could react, his world went black.

Little explosions of twinkling lights began to spread throughout the darkness. Soon the black began to fade to grey. Sam woke and took in their situation – it wasn't good.

"I really fucking hate you, Sam."

Sam was happy to hear the big man's voice. He would have felt awful if his friend had not survived.

"It's not my fault, Two Trees."

"What do you mean, 'Not my fault?'"

"Simple job. Drive a stagecoach and get paid." Sam said.

"Yet look where we are now."

The two men looked around and saw they were in deep shit. They were hanging upside down, their feet lashed to the rafters of an old, dilapidated barn. Below them were two large washtubs, and a couple of sharp knives. Their weapons had been taken and put on a wooden crate thirty feet away, but hanging fourteen feet in the air didn't get them any closer. Littered around them on the dirty floor were the remains of previous visitors to the barn. Skeletons of both men and women were in all stages of decomposition. Some were old, dried out bones, while some still had connecting tissue, and others had recently been left to rot.

The smell that wafted up to the men was nauseating, the air was filled with the buzzing of flies. All the barn doors and windows were either nailed shut or blocked by old farming equipment. Even if the men were on their feet, they'd have a hard time escaping their situation.

Sam wondered what happened to the nurse and doctor; neither was in the barn with them. If they were lucky, they had been killed outright, and felt no pain. Sam had a feeling he and his friend were going to feel a lot of pain before the day was over.

"You got any weapons on ya?" Asked Sam.

"No. My boot knife is gone along with my hunting knife and rifle."

"Ya, me too, but if I can reach the back of my neck –"

Before Sam could finish his words, the main barn door was pulled open, and the nurse was shoved in to the ground. The doctor waltzed in under his own power. "I don't deserve to be in here," he said. "I did what I was told to."

A husky voice replied. "You did, but the shipment was lost."

"And whose fault was –" Before he could finish a figure stepped into the doorway. Sam had seen a lot of weird stuff in his short life but standing in front of them was the biggest creature he had ever seen. It stayed in the shadows, but it was clearly a vampire, most likely the one that wrecked the stagecoach. Sam was blown away by the size of the thing. It had to be at least twelve-feet high and five-feet across at the shoulders.

Another shadow stepped in front of the giant vampire; this one was the size of a man.

"Perhaps, doctor, you would like to re-think our partnership. Or maybe I will."

This was the vampire that had spoken before, and it sounded like he was in charge.

"Why don't you explain to your three friends what they walked into, before we slit their throats and drink them dry." Both vampires turned and left. The door to the barn was closed and locked from the outside.

"Hey, Doc, I think you have some explaining to do," said Sam.

The doctor looked up at the two men, "Big talk from a man hanging upside-down."

"We'll see about that."

Sam reached behind his head with tied hands and found the vamps didn't get all his weapons. He pulled a small throwing knife from its sewn-in sheath at the collar of his vest. He quickly cut the ropes around his hands and then he began swinging until he was able to grab the ropes around his ankles. He cut through those bindings and then swept the blade through the rope tied to the rafters. He dropped to the floor of the barn and landed on his feet like a cat.

"I'm impressed. Where did you learn that?" Asked Two Trees.

"I learnt it from Buffalo Bill. He showed me a thing or two."

"What else you got?" Asked Two Trees.

Without a word, Sam spun on his right foot and threw the blade up. It sliced through the rope holding the big man in the air, and Two Trees Holmes did not land like a cat. He crashed down, breaking the metal washtub below him. Sam sauntered over to him and squatted down into Two Trees line of sight.

"How ya doin'?"

"Swell."

"Let me help you out of those ropes."

After Sam had Two Trees loose, he went over to help nurse Strong to her feet. The decomposing bodies and the smell of the barn disgusted her.

"Oh my God, is this some kind of charnel house?"

"More like a butcher shop."

"Are you okay?"

"No, but I will be."

"What about him?" Asked Sam, gesturing to Doctor Shane.

"Bastard deserves whatever he gets."

Two Trees walked over to the doctor, grabbed him by the collar of his suit and lifted him in the air. "Talk. Now."

Sam smiled. "I would do as he says, Doc. He's been bowled over by a horse and strung up like a piece of meat. He's not in a good mood."

Shane stuck out his lower lip and tried to puff out his chest. "I have nothing to say to y-Errk –" Two Trees squeezed the doctor's throat and smiled as the man's face started to redden and then purple.

"I would talk if I was you. He'll pop your head clean off your shoulders and the vamps won't have to bite ya."

"I – I – I'm a hematologist –"

"A what?" Asked Sam.

"He specializes in blood and it's diseases," said Alyson

"So, what do the vamps want with you?" Sam said, looking up at Shane.

"I served during the Civil War. All I saw was death and devastation. I lost so many patients due to blood loss that I've made it my goal to replace human blood with a man-made blood. So many soldiers' lives could be saved."

"And the vamps want your fake blood," said Two Trees.

"Yes, but not just the blood. They want to be able to replicate it."

Nurse Strong said, "I can't believe you've succeeded in duplicating blood."

"It works and the body doesn't reject it."

Sam thought for a couple seconds. "Two Trees, please put this asshole down. Now we know what the vamps want, why were they pissed off with you?"

The doctor sat down and loosened his tie, trying to breath normally. He was hacking and coughing, trying to drag air into his bruised throat. "I wanted to sell them the blood, but not my process. Now the greedy bastards want it all."

"But why would they want fake blood?" Asked Sam.

"They want to stop relying on humans to curb their blood lust," said Shane.

"You've got to be shitting me, Doc. Have you seen those things out there? They are as far away from being civilized as I am from being tall."

"You can say that again," said Two Trees. Sam gave his friend a quick glance and a smirk.

"I thought I could trust them. Their representative said it would be good for everyone."

"What representative?" Asked Two Trees.

"The stagecoach representative."

"Goddamn...," said Sam as he walked away in disgust.

Sam spun on the doctor. "Once they got a taste of the fake stuff, they wanted it all for themselves. Great deal you got there, Doc."

"Is that what you had tied to the back of the stagecoach?" Alyson asked.

The doctor nodded. "Yes, but once those savages started tearing the crates apart, I knew the deal went south. When the blood spilled, it drove them into a blood lust."

Nurse Stone stepped up to the doctor. "And what about us? Were we supposed to be sacrificed to those – those things?"

"My dear, it was supposed to be a simple ride out and back with a quick layover to seal the deal. I had no intentions of any of you getting hurt."

"It looks like your deal isn't happening, you stupid, little man!" She turned, crying, and fell into Sam's arms. He gently held her and caught a look from Two Trees. He couldn't tell if it was a look of congratulations or of exasperation.

"We need to leave," said the giant African Seminole.

"I'm in complete agreement," said Sam. He peeled the girl off him and went over to where their weapons had been left. None of his kit had come with the weapons so he had no powder and balls for his Le-Mat pistol. He did have one shot loaded into the shotgun barrel of his pistol, but what good was one shot? Sam found a handful of bullets for his rifle, Two Trees also had a handful of bullets. It didn't look like they were shooting their way out of there. Sam sheathed his Bowie knife and glanced up at the roof of the barn. His throwing knife was up there, embedded in the wood. There was no way he could climb all the way up there. Buffalo Bill gave him that knife. He'd miss it.

"Just let me explain it to them, I can smooth this over," said Shane. Sam looked disgustedly at the little doctor. "You're a fool. Vampires only do one thing, and that's thirst for blood. They'll take it any way they can and not care about any deal you think you made."

Two Trees grabbed Sam's elbow and drew him away.

"We must get out of here. Sunrise is too far away, and we do not have enough ammo."

"I'm fresh outta ideas. If you have something, I'm all ears."

"I have an idea, but you're not going to like it," said Nurse Strong who had joined the men.

They turned her way as she spelled out her idea. Listening to the nurse, while sneering at the doctor, the conversation went on for a few more minutes when Sam suddenly stepped away from the others.

"That's a shit idea! You're goddamn right I don't like it!"

"But Sam," said Two Trees.

"If you have something better, Sam, let's hear it," said Nurse Strong.

Sam had his hands on his hips and was staring daggers at both Strong and Two Trees. He was bouncing around any ideas he had, but nothing was going to save their asses.

"Sam, you're the only one who can do it," said Strong.

"Don't you think I know it?" Said Sam as he turned on the nurse.

"I think it's a great idea," said Doctor Shane.

Sam spun around on the little doctor. "Shut the fuck up, Doc, or I'll shoot you in the leg and leave you behind."

Sam decided to walk it off and took a spin around the barn. The smell of dead bodies and the buzzing of flies were getting on his nerves. As he walked around, he heard horses on the other side of the back wall. He continued pacing until he stopped in front of one of the kerosene lamps that lit the barn. He stared into its flame.

Two Trees and Nurse Strong decided to give Sam some time to make his decision. They both agreed that her plan was the best way for all four of them to survive the night. Neither of them was so keen on bringing the doctor along, but they couldn't just leave him behind, no matter what shitty deal he had with the vampires.

The flame from the kerosene lamp mesmerized Sam. He let himself become swallowed by it as thoughts spun through his head. He'd died numerous times since his hanging... but what might happen tonight had him more terrified than anything he'd been through.

He snapped out of his trance and took the lantern down from the wall. He walked over to where Strong and Two Trees stood.

"If, I say if, I agree to this crazy plan, what are we looking at once we get outside this barn?" He turned to the nurse. "How many vamps did you see? Were there any buildings close by?

Alyson thought a second and then looked over at the doctor. "I think I counted six, maybe seven of them, plus the giant one. What do you think, Doc?"

The doctor cleared his throat and took a couple of steps forward, saw the look on Two Trees' face and halted. "I think you're correct, nurse; I counted seven. The giant arrived later, after we woke up."

"And buildings?" Sam asked.

"Nothing that I saw," said the nurse.

"She is correct," said Shane. "There are no other buildings out there."

Sam thought about this for a hot minute. "No other buildings, too far from the mountains, and they wouldn't roost in here."

"Why not in here?" Asked Two Trees.

Sam looked up at the giant. "This is their slaughterhouse, and it's only used for one thing. There's got to be somewhe – I got it."

Sam looked at Two Trees. "Gophers."

"Gophers?"

"Yup, only other option."

"What are you talking about?" Asked Alyson, turning to Sam.

"Vamps need to sleep during the day, out of the sun. This barn has too many holes that let in light. If there are no other buildings, the only other place is underground. I'll bet there's a bunch of tunnels all under here," he said, spreading his hands out, pointing to the ground.

"So...? " asked Two Trees.

"So we need to get outta here sooner than later."

"But what about sunrise?" Asked Alyson.

"Those things aren't going to wait. They still think Trees and I are swinging meat waiting to be bled dry."

"So, we go with my plan?" Asked Alyson.

Sam looked at each one of them, and then held up the kerosene lamp. "We do, but with a twist." He had an evil grin on his face.

"Hey! Let me out! C'mon, let me out of here!"

Sam was yelling and slapping the barn doors, hoping to get anyone on the other side to open the doors.

"Let me out of here! Open the fucking door!"

"What do you want, meat?" Came the gravelly voice from the other side of the door.

"I need to talk to you. I have an offer for you!"

There was a rustling noise outside and the barn door swung out. The husky-voiced vampire stepped inside. Sam was surprised by what he saw. It looked human, but with lupine features. He was wearing dark pants, boots and a leather coat.

"How did you get down from there?" He said, pointing to the ceiling.

"Oh that? That was easy. See, I'm very talented. I could be valuable to you and your pack."

The vampire looked around the room and saw the doctor tucked away in a corner but didn't see the woman or the big Indian.

"Where are the others, your friend and the woman?"

"Oh, they're around here somewhere, probably shitting themselves with fear."

"What is this offer you mentioned?" The vampire said.

"It's simple, bite me and make me one of yours, then you get loyalty and talent all in one." Sam said spreading his arms wide.

The vampire looked at him and seemed to be considering the offer when he said, "I don't have time to train another pup. It would be easier just to drain you and wait for the next stagecoach to bring better possibilities."

With this, Sam snapped. "What do you mean better possibilities? I'm the best thing you've got coming down the road and you want to just toss me aside? He stepped forward and shoved the vampire back a couple feet.

"How dare you touch me! I'm not going to turn you; I'm going to drain you dry and twist your head off your neck!"

"C'mon, do the right thing and bite me! Make me one of you... right now!" Sam yelled.

"As you wish," the creature growled. He stepped forward with his face contorting, turning animalistic. His eyes turned yellow, his canines began to lengthen, and his nails started to become claws.

The vampire leapt into the air and landed on Sam, driving him to the ground. It grabbed his head and exposed his neck. Sam's jugular vein beat like a racehorse hitting the quarter mile. The vampire reared back, then drove its mouth onto Sam's neck, burying its fangs deep into the flesh. Sam's jugular ruptured, the blood spurting into the dead creature's mouth. Sam struggled to free himself but the creature was too strong. Its foul lips were on his skin, and he could feel its tongue lapping blood into its mouth. Suddenly the mouth stopped sucking and started to retch. Despite this, the creature went back to sucking until it couldn't take anymore and flung itself off Sam. Smoke began pouring from its mouth as sores opened around its mouth and throat.

The vampire writhed in pain, convulsing on the floor of the barn. Its screams drew the attention of the giant vampire, which quickly squeezed its bulk through the barn door. It was a hideous creature with a bald head, huge bat ears, heavy brows and a mouth full of daggers. Its body was mostly hairless, and its grey skin was scarred by scratches and old wounds. It was heavily muscled, and its left arm was winged while its right one wasn't.

It stopped when it saw its companion on the floor. Smoke poured from the ruin of its face. The open sores wept blood and fluids all over the floor, its flesh sagged and flowed from its muscle and bones.

"NO!" The giant creature roared. It bent to its companion, then looked over and saw the body of Sam lying nearby.

"I will destroy you!"

Before it could move, the doctor ran up from his hiding place and started yelling.

"No, no, it's a set up. They are hidi –"

Before Shane could finish his sentence, the giant creature lunged forward and sank its fangs into the man's shoulder. He tried to pull away, but the creature grabbed his shoulders and bit deeper. The blood lust was upon it. Crazed, it dug its claws into the doctor's shoulders and pulled, ripping him apart from his neck, down past his heart, all the way to his waist. Blood sprayed all over the creature, geysering into the air. Its thirst temporarily slackened, the vampire reared back and threw the doctor's mutilated body into a corner of the barn. It then turned its attention to Sam's body. "I will destroy you!"

Sam couldn't answer, even if he tried. His throat was torn open and the blood had already grown go tacky on his face, shirt and vest.

Suddenly stepping out from behind a wooden crate, Alyson threw a kerosene lamp at the creature, hitting it in the chest. The glass chimney broke. Hot, burning kerosene spread over the beast's chest and shoulders. It reared back as the flames spread toward its face and arms. It was about to charge Alyson when Two Trees stepped in front of her and aimed Sam's LeMat pistol at the creature's face. The nine cylinders may have been spent, but there was still the one load in the shotgun chamber. That's all Two Trees needed.

He pulled the trigger. The shotgun load tore through the creature's face and out the back of its head. Blood, brains, and bits of skull sprayed into the air and out the open barn door. The beast stayed on its feet for a few seconds, then crashed onto its back as the fire continued to burn its flesh.

Alyson looked at Two Trees. "What now?"

Two Trees took a second to decide. "Grab our gear and make sure the rifles are loaded. I'll get Sam."

"What then?"

"Shoot anything that moves. We're going around the barn to the horses."

Two Trees kneeled and looked at his dead friend. He'd heard the stories about Sam, heck, he'd seen one of Sam's "resurrections." But he wasn't too sure his friend would be coming back after this. He grabbed his friend under his arms and hoisted him over his shoulder. Sam even felt lighter. Two Trees hoped it wasn't a foreboding sign.

"Come on my friend, we have got to skedaddle before more vamps show up."

Alyson hurried past him and then stopped in the doorway. He joined her, checked his rifle making sure it was loaded. They saw that there were no vampires in sight.

"Which way?" She asked.

"To the left. Be ready to ride. I hope the horses are saddled."

Two Trees looked around. Seeing no one, he shoved the nurse ahead of him. She held Sam's rifle, ready to shoot. She was a good woman and very brave. Maybe she would come visit him at the Pretty Kitty. He would offer her a free dance and show her why some of the people at the bar called him Three Trees.

They rounded the corner of the barn and pulled up short. Four horses were tied to a tree, with two vampires guarding them. Before Two Trees could bring up his rifle to fire, Alyson had dropped all their gear and raised Sam's rifle. She shot at the vamps until she ran out of bullets. She had taken one down, outright, but the second one, only wounded, crawled towards her. Two Trees stepped in front of her and savagely kicked the creature in the face and then levelled his big Winchester at it, and shot it in the face. The vampire's cheekbone, ear and a good portion of its skull disintegrated, and its black, rotted brain started to leak out of its skull before its body even hit the ground.

Alyson stood there, rifle in hand, her head and shoulders shaking. She was slipping into a state of shock. But now was no time for weakness; it might get her killed, or worse.

Two Trees led her gently by her arm and helped her pack their belongings into one of the horses saddlebags. He threw Sam's dead body over another horse and secured it with the saddle fenders and stirrups. They both saddled up, coaxing the horses into galloping, with Two Trees holding the reins of Sam's horse. Glancing over his shoulder to see if they were being followed, Two Trees saw that the barn had caught fire. He hoped it would burn to the ground and erase all signs of the vampire slaughterhouse.

"Where are we going?" Cried out Alyson.

"Ride east!"

"Isn't Wichita north of here?"

"It is, but I would rather ride towards the rising sun, than away from it."

"That makes sense," said a weak voice.

"What did you say?" Asked Two Trees, turning towards Alyson.

"I didn't say anything."

Two Trees looked behind him and hoped he heard right. As the sky in front of them lightened and turned golden, Two Trees had them pull over to the side of a stream to water the horses and stretch their legs. He tied up his horse and helped the nurse down and secure hers. He walked back to the other horse and threw an arm over its rump and leaned against it.

"Are we there yet?"

"Nope," said Two Trees.

"Sam?" Asked Alyson.

"Hi, Nurse Strong."

Alyson ran over to Sam and threw her arms around him. Sam still lay face down over the horse.

"Are you okay?"

"Been better. Did the plan work?"

"Did you know your blood can kill a vampire?" Asked Two Trees.

"You're shitting me."

"Nope. After he bit you, he started to smoke and melted away."

"Hunh, did you shoot any of them, Trees?"

"Just the big one, after Alyson set it on fire."

Sam leaned his head towards the nurse.

"Well done, Alyson. Your plan worked."

"At least you're alive," she said.

"If this is alive, it's for the shit. Can we go home?"

"Sure thing, Sam," said Two Trees as he patted his friend's back.

"Let me help you into the saddle."

"I'm good. Just leave me here."

"As you wish."

Two Trees and Nurse Alyson walked back to their horses just as the sun crested the horizon. The small valley they were in exploded with golds, reds, greens, warm yellows, and oranges.

"I did not think I would see another sunrise," said Two Trees.

"We're lucky to be alive," said Alyson.

And from behind them: "I still hate your fucking plan."

All I had for this story was Sam and Two Tree Holmes hanging upside down in a barn. It was one of those, "Look what you got us into", moments.

As you continue to read this collection, you will find out that Sam gets Two Trees involved in a lot of weird shit. This was the first appearance of the seven-foot tall, Black Native. I had him pictured in my mind right from the start. I borrowed a bit from Craig Johnson, writer of the Longmire book series, when it came to building Two trees' character. Johnson's Henry Standing Bear is a monster of a man and also the best friend of Sheriff Walt Longmire. Walt and Henry have known each other since they were kids, and even though Sam and Two trees had not, I wanted the reader to get a feel that they shared history and a brotherhood.

Henry and Two Trees also use the same manner of speech, meaning they don't use conjunctions. This was to differentiate who was speaking in Johnson's books and if it worked for him, I hoped it would work for me.

I've used the character, Doctor Shane, in my prior novel, but this time I switched the gender and he became the asshole of the story. Nurse Strong was the love interest that Sam would never have, and then there were the vampires. Yup, I went there, but these vampires didn't wear tuxedoes, leather jackets or sparkle. What they did do is tear into jugular veins, drinking as much as they want without a care in the world. I wanted them nasty, sweaty and ugly. I also found an interesting use for Sam's blood and I thought a resurrected Sam, hanging over the saddle, hilarious. You will also notice a recurring theme: most of Sam's plans are stupid.

Love, Weird Western - Style

Sam had thought he had seen it all, but these past few days showed him he still had a lot to learn.

Friday night had come again, and Resurrection Sam had survived another week. He'd been driving supply wagons for one of the local railroad companies. His job was bringing supplies out to different work camps, off-load, and then to bring back any communications or injured men. Sam didn't mind the work; it was easy on the body and mind and he just had to have his wits about him when passing through some of the First Nation territories. He had no biases towards Indians. He enjoyed friendships with many of them, including Two Trees Holmes, William Standing Bear, and Walter Longhorn, but some of the tribes didn't like the white man travelling through their lands.

Two Trees and Sam Hawkins had met at the Pretty Kitty, where Two Trees worked as a stud to those women who could afford it. He also hired out to odd jobs to make spare cash. He wanted to pay off his contract with the management of the Pretty Kitty and end his servitude with them. It was friends like Sam that often brought him opportunities to do so.

Sam had dropped off the wagon and team of horses at the railroad office, when the breeze shifted and he caught a whiff of something downright offensive. Then he realized it was him, so he headed to his hotel room, for a bath with hot water, and a change of clothes.

Forty minutes later, Sam Hawkins, swaggering stud and resurrected man, was on his way to the Pretty Kitty for a night of drinking and, hopefully, tomcatting. He was wearing his best wool shirt, jeans, leather vest and boots. He always wore his Stetson hat and bandana, so he made sure he brushed the road dirt off them. He'd been an on-again off-again customer of the cathouse. Sometimes he stayed off in a corner by himself and had some drinks. Other times Sam wanted to do the horizontal dance with a painted cat and have some fun. Tonight, he wanted some love, so when he stepped inside the saloon, he headed over to the bar. He ordered himself a beer and a shot of rye, and then looked around for Big Laverne. She was the face of the Kitty. If you needed anything that was upstairs or out back, then you negotiated with Laverne.

Sam had a couple of favorite girls that he called upon, Cassy and Rosie. When he asked for them, Laverne said that Cassy had been reserved for the entire weekend, but that Rosie was available. She was a short spitfire with bright red hair who really liked it when Sam kissed her flower petals. Sam plunked down his five dollars and was told Rosie was upstairs in Room Four. Sam knocked on the door and a sweet Irish voice inside said, "C'mon on in, handsome."

Sam walked in and saw a most beautiful sight: Rosie was lying on her bed wearing a high corset, a lace shift and white stockings. "Howdy, Rosie. Your Sam is back in town."

"Sammy!" She cried and ran into his arms.

Rosie jammed her tongue down Sam's throat and wrapped her legs around his waist. She was obviously very excited to see him, so he turned and closed the door to the room and made sure the lock engaged.

When the door next opened, Sam was kissing his sweet Rosie goodbye, while she continued batting her eyelashes at him.

"See you soon, sweetie."

Sam's cockiness was in play, so he spun around and gave her a huge smile. "You know it, Rosie." He continued down the hall and to the stairs. He stopped at the landing and looked down the corridor leading to the special bunkhouse where some of the freakier entertainment took place. Sam was feeling so good and adventurous that he decided to see what was so cutting edge. At the door to the bunkhouse were two walking slabs of meat that were taking cover charges to enter. Sam walked up to them, nodded his hat and started for the door when a hand as wide as his chest stopped him. One of the pieces of meat said, "Ten dollars."

He looked at both of their faces and saw nothing. No anger, cruelty or evil; they were just doing their jobs. He reached into his vest and pulled out a gold eagle and flipped it to the slab that had his hand on Sam's chest. Slab #1 grabbed the coin in mid-air and the hand came down off Sam's chest, but then Slab #2 put his hand on Sam's chest and said in a hoarse voice, "That gets you in. Anything you want inside is extra."

Sam took this in, knowing he would be sight-seeing and not sampling, so he nodded. The hand came down and the door was opened. The sounds that came through the doorway were far different than what you heard when you dealt with Big Laverne for her girls. He heard a mix of yelling, laughing, screams of pain, cries of excitement, animalistic growls, jaunts, jeers and the overlying hum of voices. He stepped through the door and from behind him, both slabs of meat said, "Enjoy." The door was closed behind him.

The hall was decorated with beautiful rose and vine wallpaper, with ingrain carpeting on the floor. There were gas lamps all along the hall, and men and women were milling about drinking, talking and glancing at one another with lust in their eyes.

Sam wandered along the luxurious halls of the bunkhouse and yet, one would never have guessed what the inside of the building looked like when seeing it from the outside. From the street, the Pretty Kitty looked like a drab, grey building with large windows in the front. But the inside of the special bunkhouse was luxurious. Management had taken great care in decorating these special halls and rooms. A loud uproar of laughter and crying erupted ahead of him as a large crowd of men and women came around a corner and filled the hall. He was interested in looking around, not getting involved, so he tried to make himself as flat as he could as the crowd walked by him. Some of the men looked down to him. A few of the women batted their eyes at him, hoping to entice him into joining their group. Sam pulled his hat down and broke any eye contact.

Just as the crowd passed by Sam, he felt a presence behind him. As he turned to look, an enormous hand clamped over his mouth and he was dragged him into a room. The door was closed behind Sam, and he was pressed up against it. Whoever held him was incredibly strong and was using their larger size to press their body against him. The room only had a single lit candle; seeing who had him was almost impossible. Eventually his eyes adjusted, and he concluded he was being smothered by something firm and rough. Little sparks of reflected light danced in front of his eyes. He realized he had a face full of sequins and corset which were restricting an incredibly large bosom.

"Can't... breathe," he said. He tried to struggle but he was held tight against the door.

"Get... off."

This time the pressure on his body lessened as the figure stepped back a step. That's when Sam could see who had grabbed him. It was one of the Pretty Kitty's "mountain women". She stood over seven feet and must have weighted close to four hundred pounds. She had been shaved down and been made up to look like one of Laverne's painted women. Her skin was pale under all her body hair. She had a curly auburn wig jammed on her head and a face full of blue eye shadow, red painted lips and blush on her cheeks. She had dark brown eyes under a heavy brow, a wide flat nose, a large upper lip, a small chin and muscular jowls. She did not have much of a neck and her shoulders sloped down to muscular arms and enormous hands.

But no matter how much make-up you put on her, she was never going to be pretty or dainty.

Someone thought a tight corset was a good idea, but all it did was shove her bosom up in the air and make her look like she was wearing a tube of fabric. The corset was very attractive with the sequins and lace along the front, but they had tried to put a garter belt and stockings on her hairless, muscular legs. That just made her look silly.

Sam glanced down and saw her large feet had no shoes on them; her nails had been painted a lovely pink. He'd never been this close to a so-called mountain woman. He'd heard her tribe throughout the mountains west of Kansas hooting and crying at night, and had caught a few glances of them. He was told they were shy and timid and kept to themselves. This was a moment he would never forget.

Then she spoke.

"Yer... Sam."

"What was that?"

In a deep and breathy voice, she repeated herself. "Yer... r... Sam."

Sam put his hand to his mouth in surprise and looked around to make sure no one else was in the room.

"Yes. I'm Sam." *Holy shit* coursed through his brain. There was no way this could be happening.

"Who are you?"

She raised a large, bony hand and put it on her chest, "Loo... loo."

"Your name is Lulu?"

She nodded.

No shit.

"How do you know me?"

"Tu... Treez."

"Two Trees Holmes?"

"Ysss."

"He's a friend of yours?"

"Ysss."

"He's a good man. What do you want from me?" Sam had no idea what he could do for the big woman.

"Tu Trees... sez yu... can free me."

"Free you, from where?"

Lulu stepped back and spread her arms wide. Her wig almost

brushed the ceiling.

"Frm… heer."

"From the Pretty Kitty."

She put her arms down and slumped forward. She looked beaten and depressed.

"You want me to help you escape this place?"

Sam knew he wasn't stupid, but being grabbed by a mountain woman, in a brothel, and then asked if he would help her escape took him a few minutes to comprehend.

"Thay… hert me… heer." Lulu turned around and pushed the long wig out of the way. Sam saw her bareback and the damage that had been done. She had been whipped, cut, beaten, bruised and burned with a cattle brand.

"Fuck me," Sam said quietly under his breath. He stepped forward and raised his hand to her back. She quickly spun away, and a snarl escaped her lips.

Sam sprang back and put his hands up in a sign of surrender.

"I didn't mean anything by it. I just wanted to show you that some men could be kind."

She nodded her head and assumed her slumped stance. Sam slowly stepped forward and stood in front of her. "Look at me." She remained downcast.

"*Please*, look at me." Lulu's face turned so he could see it. He raised his hand slowly and placed it on her shoulder. She tensed, but then relaxed when she saw he meant no harm.

"I'm sorry that men have hurt you."

"Wmen… tuu."

Goddamn it.

"Lulu?"

She looked him in the eyes. Sam saw more humanity in them than he had in anyone else's face.

"I will help you escape."

Sam couldn't tell for sure, but it looked like Lulu smiled.

Sam left Lulu with his word that he would speak with Two Trees and get a plan together. He said it might take a couple of days, and with those words she became sad again. He promised that by Sunday evening, she would be on the road to freedom.

The next morning, Sam headed over to the wood and tin shack that Two Trees shared with a native woman, Aponi Maniwaki. She accepted his working situation and loved him more than anyone had in a long time. A knock on the door, and seconds later Two Trees filled the doorway.

"Hello, Sam."

"We gotta talk."

Two Trees stepped out of the way for Sam and they sat down at the only table in the well-kept and clean two-room shack. The kitchen and living area was one room, while the bedroom was in the back. Two Trees selected it because whoever built it, measured wrong and made the ceiling height a foot higher than it should have been. That was perfect for Two Trees, because at seven feet tall, he appreciated the headroom.

Aponi came out of the bedroom and went to the wood stove in the corner. She was a handsome woman with more inner strength than Sam ever imagined one person could possess. She was older than Two Trees, and had a lovely grey streak running through her hair. When Two Trees paid off his debt to the management of the Kitty, Sam was sure they would leave the territory together.

"Hat. Off."

Sam knew she was a stickler for manners, so he took off his Stetson and put it on the table, crown down so his luck would not run out.

She brought over two clay mugs of hot tea and placed them on the table. Then she kissed her forefinger, and placed it on Sam's scar.

"Nitáp." She said, welcoming him into their house.

"Miigwech," Sam said, nodding his head in thanks.

"I will leave you to speak of freedom, for my *wetompasin.*"

She left the shack on an errands run but, really, she wanted the men make the best plan they could without her presence being a distraction.

Sam took a sip of his tea and found it piney, but it turned sweet, like honey.

"You'll never guess where I was last night," he said, turning to Two Trees.

"The Pretty Kitty."

"You know?"

"Of course. Those of us who are not management are *family*. Families talk."

"Have you talked to a very tall sister, recently?"

"If you mean Lulu, yes. I spoke with her last week."

"So you know what she asked me to do, right?"

"She hinted at it, and I thought of you."

"Why on earth was I the first person you thought of?"

"There are only a few *Saskehavas* that have been taken and enslaved at the Pretty Kitty. Lulu is one of two still alive."

"I saw her back. They've beaten the shit out of her."

"That is how they work. They beat you and then beat you again until you submit. Her will is broken and she is ready to die. She only dreams of doing it with her tribe, and I felt you are resourceful enough to free her."

"'Resourceful?' I think the last time we worked together, you called it 'stupid.'"

"I may have used that word, but sometimes English words do not translate so well from Seminole."

"I got words for you that translate just fine. Fuck and you."

Sam started to get up, but Two Trees put his massive hand gently on his friend's shoulder.

"Please, do not leave."

Please... from Two Trees?

Sam sat down and drank more tea. It was starting to grow on him. He'd have to ask Aponi what leaves and roots she used to brew it.

"Why can't *you* do it?" Sam asked.

"At the Kitty, I am a piece of meat that works his debt off. I am not a free man like you."

"Me, free? You do remember my saying I've got a dead soldier looking to end my life someday. That doesn't feel so free to me."

"Sometimes, my friend, you are not so smart."

"Then school me, my friend."

Two Trees rose from the table and brought over the teapot, topping off both of their mugs.

"Have you ever thought that your Lieutenant has not killed you yet, because he is enjoying life?"

"What kind of life can he have? He's a walking dead man."

"He is, but he is also not six feet under the ground. It is not much of a life, but it is something. That is why he has not hunted you down and ended your life. If you die, he dies."

Sam thought Two Trees was full of shit, but it also made some sense.

"Do you have a plan for Lulu?" Sam asked.

"Not really, but I can give you the layout of the Pretty Kitty."

"Okay... " Sam said. "I'm in."

The two men spent the next hour formulating a plan to get a seven-foot-tall mountain woman out of a brothel.

The plan was made. Sam and Two Trees would spend all of Saturday making arrangements, separately. They decided that not being seen together would shield their friendship and Two Trees' job. They would rely on each other to have their parts of the plan in place for Sunday evening. Aponi returned from her errands and they shared their plan with her. She thought it was a good plan, but made a few suggestions on how to make it better. Neither man dared to say anything out of self-preservation.

"Do you want to stay for lunch, little *nomattimen?*"

"Will I get an invitation every time I plan a jail break?" He asked with a smirk on his face.

"You can leave now, *pigsuck*," said Aponi pointing to the door.

Sam said good-bye to Two Trees, nodded to Aponi, and left quickly. He didn't want to explain to people that an angry Shawnee woman, twice his age, had bloodied him.

Sunday was a slow day for Sam. He started out with breakfast at the Wichita Café, then took his horse, Sweetie, out for a quick ride. When he returned he took his packhorse, Larry, out for a ride, and put him through his paces. Larry was a Morgan and one of the strongest horses he had ever owned. Sam felt Larry was putting on weight and a that good sweaty run would be good for him. He wrapped up any last minute things he would need for the jailbreak that night. He began leaving a trail of his whereabouts so no one could point a finger at him for the chaos that was going to erupt.

Sam walked into the Pretty Kitty around ten that evening and looked over the crowd. It was a heavy turnout for a Sunday night and he saw a lot of unfamiliar faces. They could be anything from railroad executives bringing in prospective investors, to mining camp workers needing to blow off some steam. Sam walked by Big Laverne and tipped his hat.

"Hey, Romeo. I don't know what you did to my Rosie, but she hasn't shut up about you. Can I let her know you're here?"

Sam bashfully smiled as turned to speak to her. "Not tonight, I'm going to have a couple of drinks and walk around a bit."

"If you change your mind, and Little Sammy wants to come out and play, swing by. I'll see if Rosie is available."

"Will do, Laverne."

Sam didn't want to spend a lot of time talking to anyone; he just wanted to blend in with the crowd. He hoped it stayed busy so that Laverne would forget he had come in. He wandered through the crowd, stopped by the bar, and bought a cold beer. Nothing like a little liquid courage to get you through a prison break.

He found himself in front of the stairway that led up to the second floor and the special door leading to the bunkhouse. He walked up. The same two slabs of meat that were on duty Friday were back holding up the wall. When they saw him approach, they stepped toward him and in a repeat from two nights previous, Slab #1 asked him for ten dollars. This time he gave him two ½ Eagles. Slab #2 reminded him of the payment for extras. He smiled and tipped his hat and walked by them to the bunkhouse. Slab #2 followed him and said to his friend, "Cody, looks like our friend had so much fun on Friday, he's come back for more."

The other breathing piece of meat, now named Cody, replied. "Deacon, don't give the little man a hard time. With that face he's got to have a place to buy some love."

They both laughed hysterically as Deacon opened the door and let Sam in. After the door was closed, he could still hear them laughing. Any other time, he'd try and kick the shit out of both of them, but not tonight. There was no one in the luxurious hallway so he quickly walked in.

He reached into his jeans pocket and pulled out a carved wooden whistle that Aponi had given him. He checked to see if the coast was clear, sucked in some air, and blew the whistle. He didn't hear anything, but he felt a vibration in his head. He didn't think it worked until he heard dogs begin to howl and bark outside.

Two Trees and Aponi were sitting in a covered wagon in an alley, two blocks up from the Pretty Kitty. They'd been there for four hours. Two Trees liked to call it an *Old Indian Trick*: always be early for any meeting that might be dangerous. They had not said much of anything and saw very few people walking around. Finally, the sun set, the streets cleared, and they were left in a pleasant quiet.

They heard a sudden ruckus throughout that part of town. Dogs of every breed and size began to bark and howl. They now knew Sam was in place. Aponi looked at Two Trees with a grin and said, "Old Indian Trick." They moved on to the next part of the plan. Now it was up to Sam to get Lulu out of the building.

Sam wandered through the halls of the bunkhouse looking for Lulu, when he started hearing yelling and screaming. Then the words "Fire!", "Smoke!", and "Run!" spread throughout the halls as people began to run for their lives. Sam heard them coming, so he stepped out of the hall into an empty room to avoid the scramble. Two Trees and Aponi had set the garbage pile behind the building on fire and set up the perfect distraction. No one running for their lives, panicking that they may be burned to death, will notice him and a tall ugly woman running the opposite way. He hoped. But now, where the hell was Lulu?

Lulu waited in one of the larger rooms and saw other women run in panic, but she didn't run. It was her time to be free. Lulu smelled the smoke, and heard the sound of running feet. She needed to focus on one scent, the scent of her savior. She sniffed the air, as old instincts kicked in. Her senses shed their dullness, and she became attuned to her surroundings again. There he was, across two halls and in a side room, waiting for her.

Sam heard people running by and he knew there was no way he would be able to find Lulu in that chaos. As he began to toss ideas around in his head, he heard a loud crash in the room next door. Then there came a banging against the wall; soon it began to give way into his room. The fancy wallpaper split, the wood supports cracked, and a part of the wall exploded outward amidst a cloud of dust and smoke.

Lulu stood there, all seven feet of her, wearing a drab brown skirt, a flannel shirt and a brown wig. Gone was the make-up. Now he could see what she truly looked like. He had to admit that she looked better. Natural and wild, with a different look in her eyes than before.

She motioned to him, and he followed her through the hole in the wall and into the next. Like the previous room, this one also had a huge hole in the wall.

"You've been busy," said Sam.

This time Sam knew he saw a smirk come across Lulu's face. It seemed she liked using a little muscle.

Sam was a little disappointed that the next room had no hole in the wall, just an open door. He signaled for Lulu to hold back as he scouted ahead. Two Trees had told him about a stairway that led all the way down to the ground. Its door was marked "Private." Sam saw it down the hall, but there was an intersection and four closed doors between them and it. He sensed the mountain woman behind him, so he drew his LeMat pistol and inched forward. They made it to the intersection and saw a few people milling around at the end of the corridor. No one paid them any attention. Sam and Lulu double-timed it to the stairwell door, opened it and began going down when they heard voices below them. They stopped and remained still, hoping the people below them would leave. Seconds later they heard the door open and close, then they began to descend.

Sam peeked his head out the door and saw no one in sight, so he motioned Lulu to follow him outside. They closed the door and saw the fire in the garbage pile. It was almost burned out. Sam looked around, hoping to see his friends, but they were nowhere to be seen.

"Wht... nw... Sam?"

Sam looked up at the big woman. "I don't know. I had hoped they'd be right here." As he looked around, he heard the musical call of a house wren and spotted where the sound came from. It repeated itself, and he took Lulu's arm and brought her over to a copse of fir trees.

"Bezon nikanaki," they heard from the shadows.

"Hakiwisilaasamamo Waswasimamo?"

"Niwisilasimamo."

"Time to go, little brother," said Two Trees.

The couple moved through the trees and saw the covered wagon drawn by two horses. Two Trees held the reigns and Aponi was coming towards them. She nodded at Sam, walked to Lulu and embraced her in a sisterly hug.

"Hello, sister."

"Thnk... yu," said Lulu.

Aponi stepped back and looked over at Sam. "Don't thank me, thank him."

"Yssss."

"We need to go," said Two Trees. "We have a long ride ahead of us."

"Where do you want me?" Asked Sam.

"Up here with me. Aponi will see to Lulu in the wagon."

Sam climbed up to the empty driver's seat as the women made

their way into the back, and drew the rear bonnet closed.

Two Trees gave a tug on the reins and the horses slowly started out. They planned a two-day trip to Osage Fork in Missouri, where Lulu was originally captured. She hoped some of her tribe was still there. She did not want to die alone.

Both Sam and Two Trees had paid off Chas Samson at the livery stable, to say that he had hired them for a supply run, northwest to Kansas City. They hoped this veil of deceit was enough to turn eyes away from them and to other individuals that had problems with the Pretty Kitty.

Sam, Two Trees and Aponi all swapped out time on the driver's seat. If Aponi were up front, Sam would take a rifle and hang out at the back of the wagon, keeping an eye on their rear.

The first night on the road ended quietly. They made camp and Lulu joined them, still wearing the same clothes and brown wig that Sam saw the night of the breakout. She did not eat meat, so Aponi fixed her a dinner of vegetables and bread she had brought with them. Sam and Two Trees were given hunting duty. When they returned with a few prairie chickens and a small mule deer, Aponi butchered the animals and prepared them for roasting along with wild onions and potatoes.

After dinner, Aponi and Lulu retired to the covered wagon while Two Trees and Sam took shifts sleeping under the wagon or keeping watch by the fire.

Both men had a quiet night. Once the sun rose, they fed and watered the horses, made coffee, fried eggs and leftovers from the previous night's dinner. They ate quickly and soon got underway with the men on the driver's seat, and the women again in the wagon.

A few hours later they heard horses and voices. Two Trees asked for Aponi to come forward and Sam to go in the back to protect Lulu.

This was the first time Sam had been this close to Lulu without perfume and make-up disguising her musky scent and true face. The wagon slowed and then came to a stop. He heard an unfriendly welcome from the newcomers; one voice was more than hostile. They were speaking in Cheyenne, a language of which Sam had picked up a few choice words. He caught *"half-breed"*, *"coward"* and some insults regarding about Two Trees' lineage. Aponi spoke up for her man and the voices quieted. But then the hostile voice grew louder, nastier, and Sam again caught familiar words like *"power"*, *"rebirth"* and *"revenge."*

Sam turned to Lulu as she put her finger to her lips. He didn't know if she understood Cheyenne, but he could tell she reacted to tone of voice; this one clearly sounded evil.

The conversation eventually died down and farewells were exchanged. Sam popped his head up to take a quick look before the group left. He saw the owner of the hostile voice. An old Cheyenne, older than the others. Clearly a shaman. He had a darker complexion, thin black hair shot through with streaks of grey, a simple cord tied around his forehead and heavy brows hiding deep-set eyes. The old shaman was marked with a severe scar running through his left eyebrow and down his cheek. His left eye was a very light grey, the other, dark brown. His nose was wide and his mouth had large, flat lips. He didn't look very tall, and had the musculature of an older, fit man. Physically he did not look imposing, but he radiated an aura of power and evil. In Sam's opinion, he thought the old man looked like an ugly frog.

After the small party left, Sam could see Two Trees and Aponi relax. He shuffled forward and poked his head up.

"Who the hell wa –"

His words were silenced by Lulu's massive hand. He looked at her and she shook her head, *No*. Sam blinked his response. Two Trees shook the reins and the horses pulled the wagon down the hill. An hour passed before they stopped.

"Now can I ask who the fuck was that?"

Aponi reached out and cuffed him sharply upside his head. "Be quiet and I will tell you."

"Let us rest here and have some tea. Then we can move on," added Two Trees.

Sam and Lulu made a quick fire and Aponi soon brewed one of

her wonderful teas. As they all sat down to drink and relax, Aponi began her story.

"That was a group of powerful shamans. They are going to Onandaga Cave, southwest of St. Louis. It is a holy place for the Cheyenne and the shamans are traveling there to build their strength. The old man that you saw, his name is Matchitehew. He is a powerful and evil shaman. He is known as 'He Who Devours and He Has An Evil Heart.'"

"That old ugly guy?"

"Have some respect Sam Hawkins, even for one who is so twisted," Two Trees said.

"Okay, okay, but what was all of that yelling about? Why didn't you say anything?" Asked Sam, looking at his friend.

"My love did not say anything because the shamans do not like mixed breeds. I spoke to protect him from any harm."

"What is so special about this gathering?" Asked Sam.

"The face of Matchitehew is not his true face. He has sent his spirit forward twice. Each time he renews his strength and vigor by being reborn in anothers body.

"The body he resides in is dying, the gathering will help Matchitehew gather his strength, then the other shamans will send him forward for a third time."

Sam and Lulu sat enraptured by Aponi's story. Sam tried to understand all the spiritualism and moving spirits and was slowly grasping it.

Two Trees looked deeply into Sam's eyes. "We hid you, *nomattimen*, because Matchitehew would steal your body. Then he would never have to move forward again. He would continue to gather his strength, even if killed. He would not reside in the Camp of the Dead ever again, but merely pass through before returning. He has powerful goals. Goals which would endanger the agreements our tribes have with the white man."

"Pass through the Camp of the Dead, is that what I do?"

"Ysss, Sam," said Lulu.

He looked over at the mountain woman and realized that she was far more than just a dumb brute.

Aponi said, "the *Saskehavas* are very spiritual. Some are said to travel among the winds and visit other places. Her tribe knows of Matchitehew and is happy that he is leaving."

"Speaking of leaving, shouldn't we get going?"

"We have time, little brother," said Two Trees.

"Let me fill your tea, *nomattimen*."

"Thanks."

Aponi refilled Sam's teacup and added a few new herbs to it. He immediately began drinking from the hot cup. Clouds drifted by overhead. The warm sun felt relaxing on Sam's face, he felt better than he ever had. His body was relaxed, and the usual aches and pains from his scars were gone. He soon grew sleepy. His head sunk to his chest and he felt himself being carried on the arms of passing clouds. He was gently floating and being undressed as a soft woven fabric floated on top of him. Warming him in its embrace. He gently sighed and finally fell into a light sleep.

As he slept, he dreamt that another body settled next to him. The body was warm and comforting with a soft coat of fine, new hair. Sam couldn't focus on much of anything, a part of him did not care who was next to him.

He felt large hands running over his body, caressing his chest, neck and shoulders. He felt a fingertip trace the hangman's scar on his throat and then work its way up to the cross-shaped scar on his forehead. The hands moved down to his feet, lower legs and thighs. One of the hands focused on his cock and began tugging at it, urging his passion to rise. Sam began to move as his body responded and then the other large hand took his and directed it to a warm, moist spot and urged him to move his hand inside. He heard a sharp intake of breath, followed by a low, throaty moan.

The body next to him leaned forward and nuzzled his neck. He breathed in a heavy, musky scent that travelled through his sinuses, straight to his blood stream. It rocketed down to his hardening erection. The large body rose, straddled his cock and lowered itself down upon him. His body responded by bucking his hips, but a large hand pushed his chest down, calming him as the warm sensations spread throughout his body bringing the two lovers in sync.

Sam's head was starting to clear when his lover lowered herself down and he felt large breasts rest on his chest. An arm encircled his head, then thin lips moved along his cheek. He couldn't move with Lulu's weight bearing down on him, but at this point he didn't care. Their bodies moved together faster and faster until he felt her body shiver and tense as his passion exploded beyond anything he had ever experienced before. *Best dream ever.*

Sam woke up in the back of the wagon, beneath a quilt and a few blankets. As he started to sit up he felt a soreness through his body.

"Hello there."

He turned to see Two Trees in the drivers seat. "What's going on?"

"You woke up just in time."

"In time for what?"

"Lulu's departure."

"I'll be right there," Sam said as he threw off the bedding.

"Oh!" Cried out Two Trees, turning away.

Sam looked down and realized he was naked.

"I would appreciate it if you put some clothes on before saying goodbye."

Sam quickly dressed and joined Two Trees as they walked over to Aponi and Lulu. The women were standing together, holding hands and quietly speaking to one another. Aponi looked at the approaching men, squinting her eyes at Sam.

"Wha-she-sho-wee-ko."

Sam looked at his friend. "What the hell did I do?"

Two Trees shrugged his shoulders and remained silent.

Aponi hugged her large friend and then stood back, kissed the palm of her hand and placed it over Lulu's heart.

"Lvv... yu," said Lulu.

The women walked over to the men. Aponi walked past Sam and

scowled at him, while Lulu went to Two Trees and gave him a hug.

She turned to Sam and embraced him, resting her chin on top of his head. He chuckled and she thumped his back with her hands. She placed a huge hand over his heart, her other one on her midsection. He placed both of his on the hand on his chest, and nodded to her.

"Good-bye."

Lulu turned and walked towards the forest. She removed her long skirt, exposing her naked legs and flat buttocks. She then unbuttoned her shirt and let it fall to the ground. Her scarred back made Sam wince. He hoped the scars would eventually fade. Her bare breasts swayed as she turned to them, smiled, and removed her brown wig and threw it to the ground. Sam saw she had small ears far back on her bare, conical head. Short brown hair had started regrowing across her head, and down her neck and back.

Lulu reared back, hooted and hollered into the sky as she walked away. Her voice was incredibly loud. Sam was sure her cries would carry for miles. She continued to vocalize until, far off in the distance, she received an answer. She looked over her shoulder one last time, waved to her friends, and trotted off into the tree cover, vanishing from view.

Sam and Two Trees continued looking where she had disappeared, and then walked back to the covered wagon.

"Do you think she'll be alright?" Asked Sam.

"I do not know."

"She said she wanted to die with her tribe."

"She did, but now she might have something to live for."

Aponi overheard their discussion, as they walked closer to the wagon.

"What do you mean?" Asked Sam.

"Sam Hawkins," said Aponi, as the men came closer, "You may be my husband's brother... but you are really, really stupid."

I love this story. It came together so quickly and was exactly what I wanted it to be. I'll start out with an idea, and then I work it out in my head, like a personal mini-movie, until I think it's ready to go down on paper.

Ever since I saw the Bigfoot episode of The Six Million Dollar Man, I was fascinated by the hairy mountain men. I had to include one in this collection, and of course there had to be some 'squatch sex.

But seriously, this one came from the idea of Sam helping one of the mountain women escape the Pretty Kitty, and the story grew from there. I have no idea where the name Lulu came from, but once it popped into my head, it was perfect.

The first image that came to me, was of five-foot, five-inch Sam, coming face-to-bosom with a sasquatch. I thought it was a humorous image and I had to have it in the story. But putting the humor aside, as the story grew, so did the situation that Lulu had been put into. The story also introduces Two Trees' common-law wife, Aponi Maniwaki. She will develop into a force of nature throughout these stories. She is also torn when it comes to Sam: She'll respect him one moment, and in the next, she is calling him a "pig-dog".

This short story also pays homage to Graham Masteron's Manitou series of books with my Native American magic-maker, Matchitehew. His cameos throughout these stories are important, for they show that there are greater evils out there than anyone can imagine. It also shows my grattitude to Masterton for creating such a memorable villain as his Misquamacus.

I hope you enjoyed the sweet and tender love between Sam and Lulu. It is the first time I wrote a romantic scene and I had to be careful – my wife was going to be the first one to proofread it.

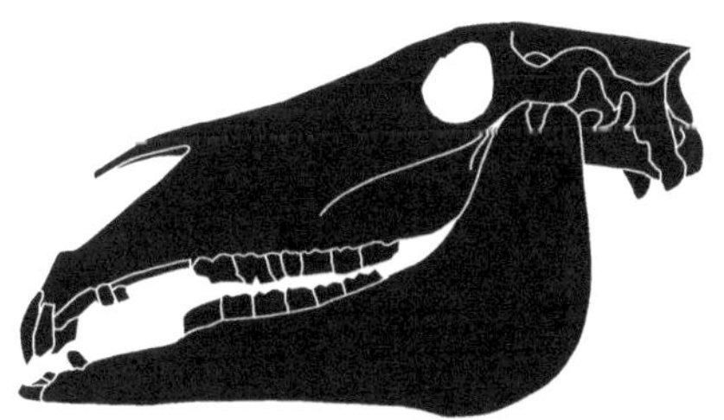

Dead Man Riding

The dead thing that had been Augustus Mace, Lieutenant in the 1st Battalion, Trans-Mississippi Confederate Cavalry, husband to Roberta and father to two young boys, sat on his undead horse and rotted in the Kansas plains sun.

It had been four years since the attempted execution of Sam Hawkins, and of Mace's rebirth. Lieutenant Mace did not feel much in his current condition. He occasionally felt hunger and would seek victims to satisfy his need for human flesh. There were times he was compelled to travel to different areas in the Kansas, Missouri and Colorado territories. He did not know what or who compelled him, but it was a pull he could not ignore. Sometimes the pull involved Hawkins and other times it seemed like he was being used as a chess pawn in some weird cosmic game. He didn't ask to become a reanimated corpse. He'd hoped his devotion to God would have been strong enough to combat the evil reanimation, but for some unknown reason, here he was, in the desert on a horse just as dead as he was. The difference was, he remembered who he was, and the dumb creature under him was only driven by hunger and the urging of Mace's spurs in its side.

Mace felt the hunger growing in his body, so he yanked the reins and the horse started down the sandy hill among the cacti and shrub grass. The small town of Binder's Bluff was due east, and it held enough warm bodies to satiate his hunger.

By the time Mace reached the town, the sun had set, and the sky was darkening. He wanted to stay out of sight, so he rode behind the buildings on the outskirts of town until he found a dark and cluttered alley. He pulled his horse up to some damaged wooden crates and dismounted. Mace slowly made his way towards the street, keeping an eye out for anyone walking his way, when he heard a voice from behind.

"You can't leave your horse there, mister. Livery stable's down the street."

Mace did not say anything nor make a move. He was hoping whoever it was would just get frustrated with the silence, and leave it be.

"Did you hear me, you stinkin' polecat? I said move your damn horse or I'll move it for you."

Mace flicked his arm out and said, "Be… my… guest."

The owner of the voice came out of a door near the back of the alley. He was fat, sweaty and waddled when he walked. He was dressed in dirty pants, a white shirt and apron. A bartender.

The man thought that this guy was creepy-weird and sounded funny, but no one tied up their nag in his alley. He swaggered over to the horse and rolled up his shirt sleeves.

"Now see here nag, I'm going to walk you out of here, and then I'm going to kick the shit outta your owner over there. How does that sound?"

As the bartender got closer to the horse, he smelled something funny.

"Hey pal, when's the last time you washed your horse, he smells like shit."

The man went around to the horse and started to take its reins.

The stench of the horse made his eyes water. "Dammit nag, I think I'm gonna puke."

The undead horse turned its head to the man, revealing the fleshless side of its face. Its dead white eye rolled around in its socket, and its decaying flesh and bone gleamed in the star light. It looked at the man and made a crude, gurgling noise.

"Holy shit, what the fuck is wro –"

That's the last thing the bartender said, as the dead horse lurched forward and bit deeply into his forehead. Blood sprayed into the night air as the horse began gnawing into the man's head until it found the sweet pink mass of brain. It took two good mouthfuls and belched.

The man tried to scream. He tried to think.

Horses don't bite into skulls, do they?

Blood ran down his face and stained his white shirt and apron. He began convulsing as the horse pulled its head back to chew its meat. The man's legs gave out, and he dropped to the alley's dirt floor.

The dead man walked over to his horse and the fresh corpse.

"I... shoulda warned ya... but screw it," he said as he looked down at the dead bartender.

He reached out and patted the dead horse's neck. Open running sores along its neck mixed pus and the bartender's blood onto Mace's gloves.

"Did ya... have a nice... snack?"

Another wet gurgle rippled out of the horse's mouth.

"Stay... here. It's... my turn.

The horse continued to chew its meal as the dead man walked out of the alley. He worked his way towards one of the nearest saloons. Mace stayed to the shadows, swivelling his dead eyes looking for a meal. Since being undead, his perceptions had changed. He now saw bodies as warm-colored shapes, and objects and buildings as grey. He took a reconnaissance position across from the Black Hag Bar and waited to see who might stumble out alone. He could easily hand two, but three got loud and messy, and he didn't want to draw any attention.

Mace was getting impatient. No decent meals. There came an un-expected squeak of a rusty door hinge behind him.

"Ola, Pedro. What are you doing on my stoop?"

Mace quickly eyeballed three men exiting a storefront door.

"Do you hear me, wetback? We don't want you loiterin' here. Why don't you and your shit-stinkin' poncho move along?"

Another man's voice chimed in. "I don't think he understan's English, Buck.

"Chesta', I do believe you're right."

Dammit. Mace was so pre-occupied with his cravings he had ig-nored the buildings behind him.

The third man spoke and poked Mace in the back with what felt like a rifle barrel. At least he knew one of them was armed.

"I think we need to give him a little push to help him off our stoop."

"Ike, I do believe you have an idea, there." Said Buck.

Buck reached out and pushed Mace's shoulder, when the dead man decided he had enough. He spun on the three.

"I'm not... Mexican... asshole."

The three men stood shocked into stillness. Mace's shriveled face with its grey, leathery skin and pronounced cheekbones, together with its sunken, rheumy eyes was bad enough. When they saw the yellowed teeth, blackened gums and the swaddling of bandage over an empty nasal cavity, their bladders let go and the shit flash-flooded from their collective assholes.

Mace seized the situation. He pushed Buck back through the open doorway, and into the darkened storefront. He pulled Ike's rifle out of his hands and swung it at Chester. The wooden stock shattered across his head and drove him down into the muddy alley. Blood sprayed from the man's head between the wooden splinters embedded in his skull.

Mace swung what was left of the rifle back at Ike, catching the man under the chin and snapped his head back. He landed on the ground with a shattered jaw and broken neck.

From inside the store came an animalistic growl as Buck charged out of the doorway with a huge knife in his hand. He slammed into the dead man, forcing him into the street. Mace shifted their weight onto his left foot and flipped Buck over his right hip. He moved swiftly, with the bigger man landing underneath Mace.

"Hi... Buck." Mace said before he drove his sharp, broken teeth down onto Buck's throat, ripping the flesh away. Mace devoured the bloody meat until he reared back on his knees, and wiped his bloody mouth with his coat sleeve.

Buck gurgled in pain and feebly clamped his hands to his neck, trying to staunch the spray of blood. His throat was ruined so he couldn't scream for help.

Mace looked around the street and saw that no one had paid any attention to the "brawl" in the middle of the street. He was sure it was a usual occurrence. Locals would conclude that two drunks were getting into it.

He looked down at Buck as the man tried to stop the bleeding and to wiggle out from under the dead man. Mace's eyes came across the large knife Buck wanted to plant in his head, and picked it up. It was a sturdy steel knife with a full tang seated in an elk horn handle. It was quite a beautiful Bowie knife, and Mace assumed his dear friend Buck must have come across it by nefarious means.

"My... Buck... that's a nice knife. I bet... it's sharp."

If the dead man's cheek and jaw muscles still worked, he would have a smile on his face, as evil as the devil himself.

He raised the knife into the air, and brought it down into Buck's chest. A small blossom of blood seeped through his shirt as the man bucked softly from the surprise and pain.

Buck... bucked, thought Mace, amused.

Mace looked into the dying man's eyes and saw no spark, no soul trying to escape, so he pulled the knife out of the chest and began ramming it again and again into the man's chest, stomach, shoulders, neck and face. Every time he withdrew the knife, pearls of blood flew into the air and decorated the mud around the two men.

When Mace was done butchering the body, he made one good kill shot into the brain. To add insult to injury, Mace reached up and tore away the cloth pad covering his ruined nose. His putrefied lungs took in a gasp of breath, then Mace exhaled, spraying the corpse with dirt, dead insects and yellow pus. He rose and stumbled out of the street. It looked like his friends Chester and Ike were still alive. Mace dragged them both into the storefront and closed the door, so he could dine in private.

Lieutenant Mace left the store via its rear exit. He stepped into an open area and saw no one around. The moon was half-full, so the shadows from his hat hid his face. He stood up straight and walked back to where he had his horse tied up. He felt wonderful, energized, ready to ride for miles on end.

Mace turned down the alley and saw his horse standing where he had left it. He looked down at the body of the bartender: the entire top of his head had been chewed away and the torso ripped open. Most of the internal organs had been eaten away, torn from where they had originally rested.

"You got... hungry."

The horse turned its head towards him as blood dripped from its muzzle. Mace reached down and grabbed the corpse's feet and dragged it back into the doorway from which it came. He listened for any voices inside the building and, hearing none, closed the door and walked back to the horse.

"Sunrise is... comin'. Time to go."

Mace pulled himself up into the saddle, took the reins in hand and directed his horse out of town. He kept to the shadows, and picked up speed as he cleared the outskirts of town. He rode for a few miles as the sun began to rise and play its warmth over his cold, dead body. He turned the horse toward a ravine that had a few overhangs. Mace pulled the horse under one of them, dismounted and let the reins go limp. He sat down, and removed his hat, revealing patches of grey skin covered with dry sores and an ever-growing bald spot. His long hair had been so beautiful. Mace leaned back and pulled his pocket watch out from under his poncho. He ran his thumb over the engraved cover and saw that soil, rust and staining had taken over. He snapped it open and looked at the fading face of his wife, Roberta. She was smiling, a wide, welcoming smile that spread all the way to her eyes. Her wavy black hair was pulled back into a bun and she had a small hat pinned to it. He never understood the purpose of those tiny, useless hats.

Macc raised his hand and touched the photo with a rotting finger. The nail had dropped off long ago and the last phalange was just starting to poke through the thin, dead skin. He traced the curve of her chin and then followed the wave of her hair. Mace dropped both of his hands to the ground and looked to the sky.

"Why, God... why?" He asked.

The undead man sat in the warming weather and looked forward to the day he would finally die. Maybe he'd get an answer then.

Zombies... I love them whether they are slow or fast. If you believe Brian Keene, then fast zombies suck. I had to do something with them, and my dead soldier, Lieutenant Mace, deserved his own story as well.

Now remember, after Mace carved the crucifix into Sam's forehead, Sam was hanged and resurrected, and some cosmic jokester thought it would be funny to curse both men with immortal life. The only rub was that Mace was now a zombie and cursed to walk the world feeding on men's flesh.

Every story must have its tragic characters, and Sam had to have a counterpart. Mace's venture into town was destined to turn bad. I enjoyed walking in his shoes and developing his agony. I guess I must be a mad god making his creations' lives horrible. Heh - heh - heh.

The Camp of the Dead

"I really don't know what to tell you, Mister Hawkins. I've never seen anything like this in my entire medical career."

Those were not the words you wanted to hear from your doctor, thought Sam.

He was lying on Doctor Walter Walters' examination table in the doctor's home office.

Sam was on his side, supported by his elbow, with his shirt and pants off. Just the lower half of his union suit maintained his dignity. Doc Walters stood in front of him and rubbed his clean-shaven chin. The doctor was of average height and trim, with a big head of light brown hair. He looked young, but Sam knew he was an established doctor before the Civil War. He had volunteered to serve so soldiers would get the best medical treatment possible. Sam imagined the doctor had seen his share of nightmares, had amputated hundreds of limbs and certified enough deaths for a lifetime.

"So let me go over this again," said Doc Walters. "You've got a low-grade fever, body aches and low energy. You can't sleep and have no appetite –"

"Yeah, I feel like shit and puke when I eat."

"How's your vision?"

"It's been fuzzy, and I went blind in my left eye."

"Are you still blind?"

"Nah, it cleared up."

"Okay, just relax while I examine your eyes." Doc Walters went to a cabinet and came back with a large magnifying glass. He examined both of Sam's eyes, lifted his eyelids and gently tapped his sinuses and orbits.

"Okay, Mister Hawkins –"

Sam interrupted the Doctor. "Just Sam, please."

"What I see, Sam, is a yellowing of your sclera –"

"What's that?"

"That's the white of your eye, and it's slightly yellow so that might mean a liver problem. Have you been drinking a lot of alcohol?"

"No."

"Okay, you have a hodge-podge of symptoms, Sam, but what I'm really concerned about, are those," he said, pointing at Sam's chest.

On his chest, upper arms, back and neck, small black lesions were scattered along Sam's skin. They were all about the size of a silver dollar, all were slightly swollen.

"Do they hurt?"

"Sometimes. It comes and goes. When it hurts, I can barely stand it."

"Okay, let me take a closer look." Doc grabbed a small stool and called for his wife, Mary to assist him. He reached over to a side table, put on a cloth gown and grabbed a cloth mask.

"Doctor, how can I help?" Asked Mary as she walked into the room.

"Sam, this is my wife, Mary. Best nurse this side of the Mississippi." Sam looked up at Mary. "It's a pleasure to meet you."

"Walt, what are those?" Mary asked.

"That is what we are going to find out. Can you tie me up?"

She came over and tied up the doctor's gown and cloth mask.

"Mary, I'd like you to also gown-up."

"Yes, Doctor."

Doc Walters began the exam by prodding a few of the lesions with artery forceps. They appeared to be infected, and wept a clear fluid. What really surprised the doctor and nurse was that when squeezed, instead of leaking more fluid, each issued a small wisp of smoke. Walters could not believe what he was seeing.

"That's kinda weird, isn't it, Doc?"

Walters looked at Sam. "Darndest thing I ever saw."

"Walter?" Asked Mary, "have you ever seen anything like this before?"

He looked up at his wife and shook his head.

It's easy to say that no one inside that room had ever heard of "ectoplasm" or believed that communicating with the dead was possible... except for Sam. He truly believed that spirits were all around them and could reach out to those individuals that were sensitive. Of course, he didn't say that to the Walters.

The doctor sat back, rubbed his chin, shook his head. "Sam are these on any other parts of your body?"

"I've got them on my back, legs – and pardon me ma'am – my ass."

"Can you roll over for me, Sam?"

"Sure, Doc." Sam rolled over onto his stomach: the same lesions had spread across his backside like a bad case of acne.

When prodded, each issued the same small wisp of smoke.

"How do these feel?"

"Same as the other ones."

"You've got an awful lot of scars here, Sam."

Sam smiled and looked over his shoulder. "Comes with the territory. And the name."

"What do you mean, Sam?" Asked Mary.

"Mary, that's his business. We shouldn't ask things like that!"

She took a step away from her husband. She wasn't used to being spoken to like that. The Walters had a very good relationship, but when it came to the medical practice, Walter was very controlling.

"It's okay, Doc. Mary, people call me 'Resurrection Sam.'"

"Why?"

"Well, I've been killed fourteen times and resurrected fourteen times."

"Like Lazarus," Mary said.

Sam looked over his shoulder, "I don't know who that is."

"From the New Testament. He was the brother to Mary and Martha. He died from an illness and Jesus took the sisters to Lazarus' tomb and raised him from death."

"So, he was one of the walking undead?"

"No, Sam", said the doctor. "He was alive and well."

"So, I guess I am like Lazarus. Wasn't Jesus also resurrected?"

"Yes, he was, Sam, but in a different way. God restored Jesus to 'exalted life'." said the doctor.

"I can say, my life has not been 'exalted'. Damn yellow bellies keep trying to kill me to prove me wrong."

"Sam, this one around your neck –?"

Sam looked back over his shoulder, directly at the doctor. "That's where they hung me, Doc. Or at least tried to. It didn't stick, so I ran off, and the resurrections started after that."

Doctor Walters pointed at Sam's head. "And that one there, on your forehead?"

"If you don't mind, Doc, I'll pass on that one." Sam said, touching the cross-shaped scar.

"Okay, well, why don't you get dressed and we'll talk in a few minutes."

"Sure thing."

The doctor and his wife stepped out of the room and into their kitchen to discuss Sam's condition.

"Walter, what the Hell are those things and what are they doing to him? He's delusional thinking he's been killed fourteen times and raised from the dead."

"Mary, I know it sounds insane, but I've spoken to at least a dozen townspeople that witnessed one of his resurrections just three months ago. He'd been shot in the chest and died in the middle of the Pretty

Kitty saloon."

"Fine, but what about those lesions? That was smoke we saw coming from them."

"I know, but there is nothing I can do for them. I could try arsenic, bismuth or mercury treatments, but the side effects could kill him."

"But he says he's immortal."

"I don't believe that, and I don't know how to understand his resurrections without being there to witness one."

"What about Pleasonton's Blue-Glass-Light treatment?"

"Total poppycock. It may work on growing plants and vegetables, but never on a person."

"What should we do?"

"There's nothing we can do. I'm going to recommend that Sam see a native shaman."

"A shaman? They're most likely to kill him before helping him."

"Modern medicine isn't going to help him. Maybe native spiritualism will. I've made my decision," said the doctor and left the room.

Sam was walking back to his rented room, when he got a bit dizzy and had to stop and rest until it passed. The doctor seemed a bit embarrassed that he couldn't do anything for him but seemed certain that native medicine might help. It didn't look like Sam had many options. Doc Walters was the best doctor in town. There were a few others around, but Sam wouldn't take his horse to them, they were so profoundly inept.

Sam thought he would go back to his room and rest, see how he felt in a day or two. He had no supply runs lined-up so it would give him a chance to sleep.

Later he'd try and eat to build up his strength.

When Sam woke up, he didn't know the time, nor what day it was. His high-fever slumber left him exhausted and disoriented. The aches that roiled through his body made sitting and standing torture. He had tried to eat, but everything that went down, came up. Weakness was settling in. Through the fog that had dropped down over his mind, he knew he only had once chance of surviving this: He had to seek out a shaman. Sam had heard of a few and some, like the Sioux shaman, Matchitehew, terrified him. Matchitehew wanted to kill all the white men for stealing his people's lands and culture.

The only two people Sam trusted who would know how to help him were Two Trees and his wife Aponi.

As Sam stumbled down the main street of Wichita, Kansas, people watched him not for who he was, but for the unstable way he walked. They also stared at the small wisps of smoke that escaped his body through openings in his collar and sleeves. It seemed like the short, blonde man was on fire, and to Sam, it felt like it. The lesions all over his body began to burn the more active he became: dressing and walking down the street was torture to him.

As he continued working his way down Main Street he often found himself in the middle of it. He did his best to avoid horses and wagons, but along the way he was clipped and then found himself down on his hands and knees.

"Can I help you?" Came a sweet voice from above him.

He turned his head and looked up into the smiling face of Mary Walters.

"I'm okay. Just trying to get down the street."

"You don't look okay. Your body is smoking, and you look unwell."

"I feel unwell. Seems my body hates me, and my little friends make it look like I'm on fire."

Mary was wearing an attractive flowered dress and a small hat. To Sam, she glowed. She knelt beside him and placed a hand on his back. Even through his denim barn coat, she could feel the fever coming off him in waves. His skin had a sickly pallor, and his eyes were sunken, the skin around them was dark. He was sweating in the early spring weather.

"Sam, let me get you back to the office."

"Doc said he couldn't do anything. Going to find a shaman."

"I still think that –"

"It's my only hope," said Sam.

"Okay then, let me help you up."

Sam nodded his head. Mary grabbed him under his arms and helped him stand. She held onto him until he had his feet.

"I'm okay."

"Are you sure?"

"Yeah, it's a walk in the park," he said and tried to give her his most charming smile. As he did, a lesion on his jaw gave up a puff of smoke. He saw the look on her face and his mouth let out the first thought that came to mind. "That was disgusting."

Mary finally cracked a smile, but he could still see how concerned she was.

"Where can I take you?" Mary asked.

Sam chin-pointed behind her. "Dobbs Mercantile."

"Put your arm over my shoulder and I'll help you walk there."

"Thank... you."

The unorthodox pair swayed down Main Street gathering looks from everyone: those walking down the street, gathering in shops and conducting business in back alleys.

"Good morning, Miss Aponi," said Benjamin Dobbs.

"Good morning, Mister Dobbs. You do not need to call me Miss, I am a married woman."

"I will remember that for next time," he said, as he had many times before, never seeming to remember.

Ben Dobbs had been in Wichita for ten years, since back when it was a rundown beginning of a town. He had the vision to start bringing in goods that the locals couldn't get elsewhere, and his business took off. He moved his mercantile from a one-room shop, that he rented, to a two-story building that he owned right in the middle of Main Street.

Ben was average height with a bit of a pear-shape, with short grey hair and a mustache that curled on the ends. At sixty years old he was still strong as a bull. He off-loaded most of the goods himself and then sorted and displayed them throughout the store. He had a couple of local teen-agers come in to help when there were large deliveries, but for the most part, it was a one-man show. Even though smaller shops had opened, he was still the largest and offered the most variety. He knew everyone and everyone knew him.

"How are my bracelets and necklaces doing?" Aponi nodded towards a display of native jewelry and trinkets that she had made from turquoise, bones, feather and clay beads. Dobbs sold them for her, on consignment.

"They are selling well, what you see is all I have left. Bring by some more and we'll price them, together. What else can I do for you today?" He asked.

"I have a small list that I can handle, but there are some supplies we need that you can help me with."

"Let me see the list, and we'll get you on your way."

Fifteen minutes later, Aponi, two parcels in hand, wound her way through town, saying hello to the people she was friendly with, and ignoring those that looked down upon her and her tribe.

Sam and Mary were almost to the end of Main Street when Sam decided he needed to go the rest of the way alone.

"Are you sure?" Asked Mary.

"Yes, I don't want to upset my friends, should they see you helping me. They put up with my malarky as it is."

"If you need our help, you know where we are."

"Thank you," Sam said, kissing her hand. She blushed and watched the odd little man stumble down the street towards Dobbs' Mercantile.

Aponi was coming around the corner of the mercantile and noticed a group of people further down the street, looking her way. She looked around but saw nothing out of the ordinary.

Sam couldn't remember when he fell in the dirt, but it wasn't long after Mary Walters left him on his own. He was doing well until he got dizzy and veered toward a hitching post. He shouldered two horses out of his way and used the post to steady himself. His vision blurred. Before long he blacked out. When he came to and realized where he was, he felt lucky that neither horse had stepped on him, but smelled one of them had pissed near him. He got to his feet and walked around the horses, patting their rear ends.

"Good boys."

Twenty paces later he reached Two Trees' home – little more than a shack – and promptly collapsed on its wooden porch.

"Two Trees? I bought some nice beef from Mister Dobbs for dinner." Called Aponi.

She heard a distant response from her husband. He was outside, behind their shack, chopping wood.

"I didn't hear you, what did you say?" She called out towards their open back door.

Just then, a sound from the far side of the front door caught Aponi's attention. She opened the door to find Sam Hawkins lying in the fetal position. At first she thought he was drunk from the night prior. When she saw the swirls of smoke escaping his clothes, she knew this was something entirely different.

"Two Trees! *Kweewa!*"

Aponi heard her husband's heavy feet come running from the back of their little home.

"Sam!" Two Trees brushed by his wife and took a knee next to his friend. He rolled Sam onto his back, exposing the black smoking lesions. Two Trees put his hand on Sam's forehead.

"He's burning up."

"Is that smoke?"

Before Two Trees could answer, Sam rolled around, moaning in pain.

Two Trees looked at his wife. "Let's get him inside."

He came through the door, with Sam in his arms, and smoke billowing around them. Two Trees laid his friend on the kitchen table. Aponi came over with a towel she had dipped into the clean water bucket they kept on the counter.

As Two Trees removed Sam's barn coat a huge cloud of smoke rose to the ceiling. He stood back, coughing the bitter smoke out of his lungs. Aponi put the cool towel across Sam's forehead. He reacted by trying to roll off the table.

Two Trees stripped Sam to the waist. The husband and wife stared at one another in disbelief. Sam had dropped forty pounds, if not more, and his ribs looked about ready to burst free. The black lesions were spread over half of his skin. Most were small, but some were as large as apples and issuing smoke from their puffy, swollen centers.

Two Trees looked at his wife. "Have you ever seen this before?"

"No, never. It must be one powerful evil spirit to have taken over his body like this. I will be back." She said, turning toward their bedroom.

Aponi returned minutes later with two dream catchers. She placed one under Sam's head. The other she handed to her husband and directed him to hang it above Sam.

Before long most of the smoke was being drawn upward toward the dream catcher.

"Will this cure him?" Asked Two Trees.

"No, my husband. This will help draw out some of the evil spirit from his body, but we need stronger medicine. He needs a curing ceremony."

Sam began to toss and turn on the table, uttering a jumble of moans, groans and words. The one the couple heard clearly, was "shaman."

"Shaman," said Aponi.

"Do you know one strong enough to cure him?"

"Maybe, but this is strong evil medicine. He may need *many* shamans."

Sam's breathing suddenly turned erratic.

"Help him, *kweewa*."

Aponi quickly made a tea of various dried herbs, salts and loose tea leaves. She filled a mug of the steaming aromatic liquid, and brought it to Sam.

She said to her husband, "Hold him up and open his mouth. We must make sure he drinks enough of this tea."

It took some time, and they made a mess, but Sam finally drank the entire mug. Eventually his breathing slowed and evened out, and his body noticeably started to relax.

"What was that?" Asked Two Trees.

"Something to make him sleep and ease his mind. He will sleep deeply. I hope it gives me enough time to bring him to the right people."

The next day Aponi and Two Trees set out northwest to find a small tribe mainly made up of medicine men and shamans. They rented a buckboard wagon from the livery stable and arranged to have it back in a week. Two Trees had told Big Laverne at the Pretty Kitty that he would be gone visiting a sick family member. She wasn't happy, reminding him of his contract and of how much he still owed the saloon. The large Indian apologized for the short notice; it was very important.

Aponi had heard the tribe lived in the Horsethief Draw range of mountains near the Colorado border, north of Weskan. Two Trees estimated it would take them three days to get there. He hoped Sam wouldn't die, along the way.

The first day on the road was uneventful. Aponi would ply Sam with more of her special tea as Two Trees drove the wagon. The two would occasionally switch, and Two Trees would sit and talk to his friend, hoping Sam was listening. He realized how much he loved his brother. At night, they would alternate sleeping in the wagon with Sam while the other slept underneath. They had enough supplies for a full week and if they needed anything special, Aponi was a good hunter.

The second day saw them hit random rainstorms. The cold water set off Sam's chills. Aponi had hoped the cool water would reduce his fever. She fed him mashed meat and vegetables and, for the most part, he would eat. Still, there were times that he could not keep any anything down.

Early on the morning of the third day, Aponi sat away from the two men and the wagon. She began burning sage in order to clear away her thoughts. She reached out with her mind, and tried to contact the shamans they were searching for. After exhausting herself for hours, she rejoined Two Trees. In mid-afternoon they came upon a small figure walking their way. A man, barefoot, dressed in light woven wraps in different hues of orange. He had a shaved head, his face was painted with white clay and his eyes looked like two black marbles.

As they pulled up to him, he bowed, and Aponi repeated the gesture. The little man's attention was drawn to the back of the wagon. Aponi allowed him to peer in at Sam.

"*Paúsawut kitonckquêwa*. I think two days, no more," He said, in a very deep voice.

"I am Aponi Maniwaki of the Shawnee. This is my husband, Two Trees Holmes. We are searching for the Abbomocho, the healing tribe."

The little man stepped onto the buckboard and threw the quilts off Sam, exposing his withered body. The lesions had spread further, and the acrid smoke continued leaking into the air.

"He is sick with *Matche Mundoo*, the Spirit of Evil. How many times has he come back from the Camp of the Dead?"

Two Trees was shocked by the question. The stranger can't have known who Sam was or what his peculiarity was.

"How do you know that?"

"How many?" The little man gave Two Trees a sharp look.

"Fifteen, maybe seventeen times."

"That is too many. He brings back evil Manitou with him every time."

"What can we do?" Asked Aponi.

"You have done everything you could to get him here. Now I need to bring him the rest of the way."

"We want to be with him. We are his only family," said Two Trees.

The little man scowled slightly, and then looked back at Sam.

"I drive wagon, you two sit in back."

"Who are you?" Asked Aponi.

He looked at her and smiled, his face lit up with an abundance of energy. "I am Wanageeska, The White Spirit."

"Sioux tribe?" Asked Aponi.

"No longer. When you join Abbomocho, you are no longer who you were. You are now a spirit."

Two Trees and Aponi exchanged questioning glances. They joined Sam in the back of the wagon, as Wanageeska took the reins and directed the horses off the road into a small copse of trees. As they drove further into the trees, the smell of fresh blossoms filled the air and petals floated along the gentle breeze. The rocking of the wagon and the perfume from the trees helped Aponi and Two Trees relax. Soon they drifted into a gentle slumber. No wonder; they were utterly exhausted.

When they woke, they found themselves in the middle of the Abbomocho camp, and saw that Sam and Wanageeska were both gone. The horses had been unbridled and left in a small corral with other horses.

A large fire pit dominated the center of the camp, where two women roasted a spitted deer. A dozen small teepees surrounded the pit and a few older shamans walked about in small groups. Behind the teepees was a larger tent encircled with boulders. A second large teepee was off to their left and was decorated in red paint, symbols and representations of warriors and animals. Protective arrows, wise crows, the dancing man, ceremonial drums, the great spirits higher power eye, the eight-pointed star, the eyes of medicine men and the powerful thunderbird were all represented.

Behind them, Wanageeska reappeared holding the two dream catchers that Sam had arrived with. Both were black with mold, and stank of evil and sickness. He walked them over to the large campfire and tossed them in. To the normal eye, nothing came of it except some popping of embers and a flash of fire. But those with the sight, like Wanageeska, saw evil spirits screaming into the sky with nowhere to go. Each would fade away and die without a human host to take over.

"He is in there," said a voice from behind them.

Aponi and Two Trees turned in unison and found themselves facing a tall, thin man of incredible age. He had long white braided hair that ran down his back, and a deeply lined face. He wore a simple loincloth and an elaborate necklace of turquoise, bone and feathers.

"I am Kajika, He Who Walks Without Sound. I welcome you to Abbomocho."

"Hello, I am –"

"I know who you both are. I am glad you brought your friend to us."

"Can you help him?" Asked Two Trees.

"We will see. It will be a few hours before we start the Cleansing Ceremony. Would you like something to eat?"

The couple looked at each and nodded. "Then follow me," Kajika said.

They were led to a small area away from the main camp and directed to sit around a small fire. They were given cooked root vegetables and smoked venison. They ate slowly and kept their eyes peeled for anything out of the ordinary. They saw a few older men walk about camp followed by larger, stronger looking men and women. The latter seemed to act as aids, yet gave off the vibe of being bodyguards. Two Trees took it all in as calmly as he could, while Aponi was on pins and needles. He could not understand her fear. She said it was because he had never studied the medicine, nor had the experiences she had.

Time slipped by, and as the sun chased clouds and its sister the moon westward, the sky began to darken.

Kajika appeared behind them like a ghost, living up to his name. He told them the Cleansing Ceremony was almost ready and they could follow him to the Spirit Teepee.

Outside the teepee waited the aides - slash - bodyguards to the shamans whom they saw walking around the camp earlier. The most highly revered men were nowhere in sight, so the couple assumed they were inside, preparing the ceremony.

Kajika pulled aside the flap of the teepee and the three of them entered.

Inside was dark, solely lit with small lamps containing bear grease. At least a dozen ancient shamans sat around a central raised platform, beneath which glowed a bed of red hot coals. Water was being dripped onto the coals to create the steam. It would bring on the sweat needed to cleanse their bodies. Bear and deer hides were tacked to the sides of the teepee; all had symbols and icons scraped into the fur. Aponi smelled sage in the air along with the grease from the lamps. She also caught traces of cinnamon, coal, body odor, and the sharp tang of fear. Kajika gestured to two empty spots on their right. They sat down.

Two Trees removed his flannel shirt, exposing his developed muscles, auburn skin and scarred back. Aponi removed her hide shirt exposing her naked breasts and scarred icons on her shoulders. A few of the shamans seemed uncomfortable with a half-naked woman among them, but Kajika nodded his head, and they accepted the situation.

At the head of the raised platform sat a shaman wearing a vest of feathers and fur, and a mask carved from wood. The mask had large carved eyes and a sharp, narrow nose that looked more like a beak. The lips and mouth were carved into a smile, and eagle feathers were painted on the jowls. A large black feather rose on each side of the mask and a group of wide white feathers spread out from one side of the mask to the other, creating a mane.

Two assistants sat to each side of the older shaman, waving woven fans to draw the scented smoke closer to the masked shaman's face. His chest rose and fell slowly as he took in the smoke and steam.

Two other aides rose from behind the shaman. They stepped forward and grasped the blanket that lay across the platform. They removed it with a flourish, revealing the body of Sam Hawkins.

"Sam!" Yelled Two Trees, rising to his feet. It's unsure if he called his friend's name from the surprise of seeing him, or from seeing the condition of his naked body. His skin was paler than usual, and he had lost more weight. The lesions had continued to spread across his body, and in some places, as on his torso, the skin was more blackened than not. On his body and face, icons and symbols had been painted in red paint. Across his chest was drawn the thunderbird symbol, and

along his arms were the circles that represented the cycle of life to death and rebirth.

On his forehead, around his cross-shaped scar, was painted the four-pointed star that described the Leonid meteor shower of 1833. The original people considered it the year the stars fell. Running down his legs were arrow symbols that represented protection and defense.

Once again Kajika lived up to his name, and appearing silently beside Two Trees. The shaman placed his hand on the giant's neck. That simple act of gentle pressure comforted the man, and he sat back down. Aponi was amazed by her husband's reaction and the unseen power held by Kajika.

She looked around the teepee and recognized some of the other shamans. To her left was Hamatsa, wearing a crown of carved wood and tree limbs. Next to him was Taqui, a Moki Sanke priest, whom she thought had been dead for ten years. Across from them, shaking two gourd rattles, was Angkok. Next to him were Black Elk and his son, Fools Crow. Both were adorned with feathers and red lines across their noses. Black Elk wore a bowler hat and smoked from a long pipe. For Aponi, this was an experience of a lifetime, a moment in time she would never forget.

The ancient shaman wearing the bird mask began to bounce in place in time with the rattles. He then raised from his side the largest bone Aponi had ever seen. She thought it was a human femur, but it was twice the normal length. It must have come from one of the mountain men tribes. It was very old and had a string of feathers, beads, and smaller bones hanging from one end. He began to strike it on the ground, its beads and bones jangled together. All the shamans turned their heads to the elder and grew quiet. He rose to his knees and began to chant and sing about the healing power shared by all. How it needed to be turned towards Sam, cleansing him while keeping Malsumis, the cruel, evil god, from crossing over and taking their world.

Between the chanting and singing, Aponi heard him say a name, Rolling Thunder. An old shaman she knew to be dead, yet here he was in front of them.

Rolling Thunder stopped chanting, cleared his throat, and spoke in the language of the white man, for it was a white man they needed to help.

"Brothers, this man has strong evil inside him. He has travelled to the Camp of the Dead and returned many times. Too many times! He brings back evil each time. This evil has grown inside him and is fighting him to get out. He is losing." Rolling Thunder pointed to Two Trees and Aponi.

"Two Trees Holmes of the Seminoles and Aponi White Feather of the Shawnee are this man's family. We thank you for bringing him to us. Without you, he would be dead, and the evil would be in our world."

The couple nodded in thanks. Behind them, Kajika motioned to two of the aides, who then moved in behind Two Trees. They were the biggest and strongest among the groups. He hoped they would be enough.

Rolling Thunder continued. "Sam Hawkins travels between here and the Camp of the Dead and he must be helped." Rolling Thunder dropped his hand to his side and grasped a stone knife that was hidden there. He raised it and with every ounce of his energy and drove it straight into Sam's chest.

"No!" Screamed Two Trees.

The two aides sprang forward and did their best to restrain him. Two Trees weighed over three hundred and fifty pounds, and although the two smaller men did their best, it simply wasn't enough.

Two Trees tossed one man to the side and the other backwards into Kajika, who had stepped forward to calm the giant. Before he could make a move towards Sam and Rolling Thunder, Aponi touched his shoulder.

"Husband, it is alright."

He turned his head and looked at her. "What do you mean? He stabbed Sam!"

Aponi put her hands on his massive shoulders, and felt the strength rippling through them. If left to his own, he would kill every shaman in the teepee and tear it down to the ground.

"This is how it is supposed to be."

"I–I don't understand."

"Sam has to return to the Camp of the Dead and leave behind the evil spirits that have attached themselves like ticks."

"But–"

"It is the only way. He must die, to go back," said Aponi.

Two Trees looked at his wife, and then back at his best friend. Tears started to flow down his face. His entire body shook in anger, fear and sadness.

"Two Trees?"

The giant turned to face Kojika. "Stay in peace or leave this place," said the shaman.

Aponi stepped forward and hugged her husband. "It is the right thing to do."

"Yes."

Giant femur in hand, the ancient shaman, Rolling Thunder, once more began his rattling just as an aide poured more water on the hot coals.

Two Trees sat back down and stared at the steam rising and encircling his dead friend, hoping that his resurrections had not ended.

Sam found himself walking through mist toward a small Native American village. Everything around him appeared off. The colors of the trees, the teepees, even the bonfire in the middle of the village looked washed out. A constant breeze swirled the mist about and at times a sound like that of an approaching steam train rode upon the wind. He could not see the sky or the sun. All was enveloped beneath a gloomy grey cloud.

Ahead of him a dozen teepees stood surrounding the bonfire. All sorts of natives wandered about. He watched as warriors, farmers, squaws, old men, and even children, walked out of the mist and into the village. Some wandered aimlessly, while others stepped purposefully into teepees. Some strode directly into the bonfire, screaming. As they did so, the colorless flames would swell, engulfing them, yet when the flames receded, they were gone.

Sam believed that this was the Camp of the Dead that Aponi often spoke of, the place she believed Sam visited every time he was died.

A small man with soulless eyes walked past Sam, moaningly deeply. Sam followed the strange little man into a teepee, but upon entering, Sam found it empty. He turned around inside the teepee yet found no other exit.

A new sound crept into the camp, echoing throughout: That of bones being broken, of fingers being snapped and ribs being crushed and splintered. From out of the mist a creature of nightmare reared high into the sky. Four tall legs covered in fine hair carried a long body that together reminded Sam of an insect. The monster's face however was something else entirely. Smoky breath flowed from a mouth of needle-like teeth set within a head reminiscent of a horse's skull. Empty eye sockets blazed red with an evil never before seen by the living. A long wispy mane flowed from the top of its head down along a bony spine.

And it wasn't alone.

Within moments three more of the creatures ambled into view, joints snapping and popping with every movement. They were known as the Crackling Dead, devourers of souls, seeking out trespassers and travellers passing through to other dimensions and time lines.

Sam saw the other souls wandering the camp had run off or were in hiding. He reached down for his LeMat pistol and found himself naked, the lesions gone from his skin. He stuck out his arm and saw that someone had been busy drawing tribal icons on his body. He also found a weeping wound over his heart and wondered where it had came from, but this was no time for thinking.

The closest creature lunged forward and swung one of its spindly legs at him. Sam dove safely away below it but felt both the chill that it threw off, and the sting of its wispy hairs as they brushed his back.

Sam got to his feet, as another Crackling Dead charged him from behind, ramming him with its broad horse-like head. Sam was thrown through the air, over the bonfire, and crashed into one of the teepees. The creature charged forward, but realized too late that it had stepped directly into the bonfire. Thrashing to escape, the panicked monster instead entangled itself amongst the fire's many logs. Bellowing in pain and rage, its howls soon devolved into pathetic unanswered mewling, cries for help. Within moments the dead thing had collapsed into itself, no more.

After the creature's cries had faded, the other three refocused their attack on Sam. He was promptly pawed, kicked and thrown around the camp. As he laid on the ground with blood running from his mouth and new bruises forming on his limbs, one of the creatures stood over him and opened its mouth, roaring in triumph.

Just then, a large hairy hand struck the monster in the head with a burning log. The creature roared in anger.

Who? Wondered Sam. *Who is this helping me? Could it be? It is!*

"Lulu!" Sam cried out.

But the mountain woman – also known as a Sasquatch – and one-time lover to the beleaguered Sam, ignored him.

Instead, she charged the creature and struck it on the head again and again until a flash of fire and sparks exploded from the club. The hellish beast fell to the ground, howling. Lulu was on it in seconds and resumed clubbing it over its head and face. She then shoved her burning club through one of the creature's eye sockets, into its skull until the thing stopped moving. It was only then that Sam noticed that Lulu had a papoose carrier strapped to her back, and inside was a little furry mountain child.

The remaining Crackling Dead came together and prepared to square off with the Mountain Woman and the injured man. Lulu positioned herself between Sam and the creatures and then quickly backed up to Sam, chin gesturing to her child. Sam picked the baby out of the papoose carrier and held him to his chest, backing away from both mother and monsters. Lulu smiled and turned back to the creatures, charging at them, waving her burning club.

Sam watched as she swept through both of them, letting her animal side come out. Although the Crackling Dead did manage to strike her with their long-limbed arms and legs, Lulu was a mother protecting her child. Lulu's roars echoed throughout the camp, mingled for a time with the snaps and cracks of breaking bones. Within minutes Lulu stood over the mangled, broken bodies of the two Crackling Dead. The crackling was over, replaced by the low moans of their souls, adrift on a breeze.

All during the battle Sam held the child close, at times struggling with his weight. The boy – for there was something very male about the child – was at least three feet tall, and all elbows and knees. As the child stared at the crucifix shaped scar upon Sam's forehead, Sam took the time to look more closely at the boy. He was clearly different from other mountain children, for his head lacked the conical-shaped skull of his mother and her people. His hair was much finer and not brown, but blond. Besides having blond hair, the child also had dazzling blue eyes that Sam quickly recognized as his own.

Lulu dropped the club and came over to Sam and the child. As soon as he saw her, the child reached out to his mother, and she scooped him up in her arms.

Lulu looked down at Sam. "Hello... Sam," she said, somewhat bashfully.

"Hi, Lulu. I'm happy to see you."

"Me... too."

Her child looked at Sam and made gurgling noises with his lips.

"He's quite a handful."

"Yes... he is. He... takes after his... father."

"What's his name?"

"Hawk."

Sam leaned forward and touched the boy's arm. "Hello Hawk, my name is Sam."

Hawk reached out and patted Sam's forehead scar with his dark brown, leathery hands.

Sam looked up at Lulu and asked, "What are you doing here? How did you know I was here?"

She had so much to say, but still lacked the language skills to convey her thoughts.

"I knew... you were... healing teepee 'cause Rolling Thunder... has my founder's bone."

Not understanding her, Sam just nodded.

"But here?" He asked, gesturing around them.

"My tribe... can... walk from place... to place. My shaman... sent me... here to help."

"But why me?" Asked Sam.

Lulu looked at Sam and then to Hawk, and Sam had his answer. For only a few times in his life, he was again speechless.

"He will be... leader... someday."

Sam smiled. "I'm sure he will."

Hawk looked at his mother and took her necklace and put it in his mouth. Then he turned his gorgeous blue eyes towards Sam, and smiled a toothless grin.

Sam chuckled and rubbed the boy's fuzzy blonde head.

"You... have to leave... here," said Lulu.

"Fine with me, how do we do it?"

"You... have to... burn the evil... from you."

"Oh, I don't like the sound of that," he said, looking at the bonfire.

"It's going to hurt, isn't?"

"Yes..."

"Yssss..." Said Hawk.

Sam looked at the boy and smiled, with both pride and affection. He looked up at Lulu, stepped forward and gave them both a long, heartfelt hug.

"Let's get this over with," he said, pulling away.

The three of them walked to the bonfire. It immediately flared high into the sky.

"It looks like it knows I'm here."

"You will... be fine," said Lulu.

Sam noticed they weren't alone anymore. The ghostly people had begun to enter the camp again, now that the threat of the Crackling Dead was over. Instead of following paths of their own, they all gathered around Sam, Lulu and Hawk.

Lulu took Sam's hand and smiled. Her face was so different now than when he had first met her, but he still saw the beauty there. Sam winked at Hawk, turned and walked toward the bonfire. The gathering of souls crept in closer as he reached the bonfire. He told himself not to look back. He reminded himself that Lulu and Hawk would also return to the land of the living, they would be fine. They had come to the Camp of the Dead to help save him, perhaps risking their lives, if not their souls. He would be forever grateful.

Before stepping into the fire, Sam took one last look around. Many souls had gathered to watch Sam's progress, but only one did so with contained malevolence. There, behind the nearest teepee stood Matchitehew, the most powerful shaman known to the native tribes. He was smiling at Sam. *Did he know of Sam's resurrections?* This is what Aponi feared most. That the evil Shaman wanted Sam's seemingly immortal body for his own.

Sam flipped him the middle finger, and stepped into the bonfire's flames. Pain seared through his entire nervous system. He thrashed and screamed in agony as the evil that had piggybacked into his plane of existence, were expunged from his body. They would forever burn in the bonfire of the Camp of the Dead. Never again would they know peace or be able to infect wanderers with their filth and desires. Sam's screams began to falter as the fire ravaged his throat, and as blood sprayed from his lips. The painted icons on his body faded away, but one scar, the cross on his forehead, burned brightly, causing the gathered souls to turn away from it's intensity. Even Matchitehew turned away for fear that he would be blinded. The light grew in intensity until it fully obscured the Camp of the Dead.

Two Trees and Aponi stayed in the sweat teepee even while aides saw to their shaman's needs for food and drink. Kajika had brought the couple hot, spiced tea to keep up their strength and retain their focus. The only figure that did not move or take nourishment was Rolling Thunder. The old shaman had yet to cease beating the ground with his bone staff or quit chanting, even though his voice had been reduced to a hoarse whisper.

Sam's body remained unchanged. The stone blade had been pulled from his chest, and a wad of woven fabric placed over the wound to sop up the remaining blood.

Suddenly, Rolling Thunder's chants increased in volume and strength, and as they did so Sam's lesions dried up and faded away.

"*Munumayenok*, look." Said, Aponi pointing at Sam.

Two Trees saw the changes in his friend's body. Sam was now starting to sweat, his ashen skin regained its color.

Suddenly, the resurrected man sat up and screamed, as though waking from a cruel and terrifying dream. He looked around in confusion, gasping and shaking. He felt a pain in his chest, noticed the wad of cloth placed there, and pulled it away to see the healing wound.

He looked around the teepee and in a shaky voice said, "Who the fuck stabbed me?" A moment later, his eyes rolled up into his head and he fainted.

Sam and the Holmes' stayed at Abbomocho for two days, and in that time Sam had been poked and prodded by most of the elderly shamans. Especially by Aponi. He assumed this was at Two Trees' urging. He was well fed and his energy was coming back. He had slept well after his resurrection and was able to walk on his own around the camp without any of the shaman's aides assisting him.

On the morning of the third day, Sam, Two Trees and Aponi packed the buckboard with supplies given them by the camp: dried meats, salt preserved vegetables, loaves of fresh bread and bottles of a homemade spirit from the saguaro cactus called *haren a pitahaya*.

Sam was given a fresh set of native clothes made from the softest deer hide he had ever felt. He missed his hat, which he hoped was still in his room back at the hotel in Wichita. Wanageeska gave him a hat left behind by an earlier camp visitor. It would keep the sun out of Sam's eyes while covering his scar.

Rolling Thunder declared that the cleansing ceremony was successful – Sam was rid of the fragments of evil spirits that had travelled within him. One of Rolling Thunder's aides gave Sam a bear fetish carved from blue anhydrite. He was told it would protect, heal and transform him so long as he kept it with him at all times. If he were killed again, the fetish would ward off any evil spirits, he would not have to go through another cleansing. He thanked the aide and nodded in the direction of Rolling Thunder.

After the farewells had all been said, the threesome loaded their wagon and began the trek back to Wichita. This time, the little man, Wanageeska, walked them out to the edge of the camp, letting them ride out on their own. Aponi felt this was their way of saying they were trusted and welcomed back to Abbomocho in the future.

Sam slept over the following days until he felt he was ready to take his part in driving the horses. He joined Aponi on the bench, asked her for the reins and said she should rest in the wagon with her husband.

This left Sam to his thoughts for many miles and a chance to take in the bright sun and feel the gentle breeze on his skin. He hadn't felt this good in years. As he looked to the sky he saw sparse cloud cover and a lone raptor cruising along the higher winds.

Later in the day Aponi joined him on the driver's bench.

"Have a good nap?" Asked Sam.

"Yes, I was very tired."

"Good."

"We haven't had a chance to talk about what you saw –"

"When I was in the Camp of the Dead?"

"You where there?" She asked.

"Ycs."

"What was it like?"

"Terrible."

"Can you tell me –?"

Sam grew quiet and then said, "I saw Matchitehew."

Aponi jerked her head around and looked at him in surprise. "In the Camp of the Dead?"

"Yeah. He was hiding behind a teepee."

"Did he see you?"

Sam looked at Aponi. "Fucker even smiled at me."

"I'd hoped he was dead. Did you tell Rolling Thunder?"

"I did. He seemed like he already knew the bastard was alive."

They both sat in silence, considering the implications. Two Trees, still asleep in the back of the wagon, started to snore. Sam looked over his shoulder, shocked by the shear explosiveness of the snores.

"Does he –?"

"Every damn night."

They broke out in laughter. Two Trees slept on, not missing a beat.

Sam regained his composure and blurted out, "Lulu was there."

"She was?" Asked a surprised Aponi.

"She saved me."

"How did she even know you were there?"

Sam looked at Aponi. "Do you remember the staff that Rolling Thunder carried?"

"The bone?"

"Yes. Lulu told me it belonged to one of her ancestors, and that *he* told her I was in the Camp."

Aponi was surprised by the answer. "His Manitou still lives in the bone staff."

"I guess it does."

Sam had a smile on his face as he thought about Lulu saving him.
A serious look came over Aponi's face. "Was she alone?"
"No."
"Was she with a child?" Asked Aponi.
"Yes."
"And –"
"His name is Hawk –"
"Oh."
With a huge smile and a tear in his eye, Sam looked at her, "–and he's beautiful."

Something kept nagging at the back of my brain: where did Sam go when he died? I didn't know much about the Native American afterlife, but after researching it, I found the Camp of the Dead. The Crackling Dead are my own creation, and were inspired by the creepy hallway ghost from the movie, Poltergeist.

All of the shamans were based on research into real-life medicine makers. There never was a village made entirely of them, but wouldn't that have been amazing.

We are introduced to the Walters, Walter and Mary, our town physician and wife. Why Walter Walters? My research found this was a common practice during the 1870's. I guess creative child naming came a bit later.

I'm very happy how this story came about. It developed how I imagined it would. I'll be honest and say that I brought back Lulu because I liked her so much; I didn't want to say goodbye.

Raptors

There is just so much love and attention one man can take, and Sam Hawkins had reached his limit. He appreciated all the soups and teas that his friend, Aponi Maniwaki, prepared for him, but his stomach was as full as his bladder. Sam also loved his friend, Two Trees Holmes, but he watched Sam almost every minute they were together, and Sam was feeling smothered.

Sam split his time between his rented room at the hotel and the Holmes' shack, but he felt the need to head out to the desert.

When he and his friends returned from Abbomocho, the healing tribe, Sam had stopped in to see Doctor Walters and his wife Mary for an examination. Doc was surprised to see him. Sam's condition had been so grave Walters assumed he'd died.

"How are you feeling, Sam?" Asked Doc Walters.

Sam was seated on the examination table with his shirt off, Doctor Walters was behind him, examining his skin and thumping his back.

"I feel great, Doc. I'm sleeping well and Aponi is making sure I'm well fed."

"But Sam – how is it you're alive?"

"I took your suggestion and found a shaman."

"It really worked?"

"Well, we found an entire tribe of shamans, but yes, they healed me."

"Can you tell me how?"

"It's an awful long story, Doc. How about we talk about it some other time?"

"Okay." Doctor Walter Walters was originally from Philadelphia and graduated top of his class from Penn Medical School. He took great pride in his advanced medical training and instruments. When he received his first stethoscope, he was delighted and used it at every opportunity.

"Alright Sam, let's take a listen to your heart and lungs."

As Walters was working, his wife Mary, walked into the examination room.

"Walter, I wanted –"

"Hello, Mary," said Sam.

"My God, Sam Hawkins. I thought you were –"

"I very nearly was."

"Well, Sam," said Doctor Walters standing up and putting away his stethoscope. "Your lungs are clear, and your heart is beating strong. I see you have a new scar on your chest... "

"That's part of the long story."

Sam hopped off the table and started putting his shirt back on. "If that's everything, I'll be heading out."

Mary asked, "You're not going to do anything dangerous, are you?" Sam looked at her and mocked being offended. "Me, dangerous? Of course not. I'm going for a long ride with my horses just to get away from town. I should be back in a few days, and then I go back to work driving for the mine."

"Just remember, Sam," Doc said, "your body has been through a lot so don't overdo it."

"Doc, don't you worry. It's just going to be me, the horses, some sand and the sun."

Sam walked out of the doctor's office with a quick wave back and headed up the street to the livery stable.

"Walt, how is it that Sam's – "

"I'm sorry, Mary. I have no idea."

Sweetie was thrilled to see Sam. She just about burst out of her corral when she saw him come into the stable. He slipped her a long carrot to keep her busy while he walked over to his packhorse, Larry. As he rubbed the big Morgan's head, Larry fluttered his lips and Sam gave him an apple from his pocket.

"Who's a good boy?" The horse didn't respond. He was too busy sloppily chewing his apple and spraying juice all over the railing. Sweetie had finished her carrot and was nodding her head at Sam. He knew she was trying to sweet-talk him into another carrot, which he had stashed in his vest, but he wanted her to work for this one.

He pointed to the ground in front of her and stamped his foot and then waited. Sweetie looked at him, bowed her head, and stamped her foot three times.

"Good girl. Now here is your reward," he said as he gave her the carrot. She gobbled it right down. Sam packed the saddlebags that Larry would carry. All his food, grain, and alfalfa would be carried by the packhorse, while Sweetie's saddlebags would carry his extra clothes and the ammunition for his weapons. He would only be gone for a few days, but he liked to over-pack because weird things always happened to him. Always.

Sam walked the horses out of the livery stable followed by Charlie Reynolds, the stable boy, carrying a pitchfork and a bale of hay.

"Taking off, Mister Hawkins?"

"Hey, Charlie. Going out to the hills for a few days. I need some alone time."

"No problem, I'll be here when you get back. It'll give me a chance to clean out Sweetie and Larry's stalls."

"Thanks, Charlie," Sam said as he swept up into Sweetie's saddle.

Charlie was a good guy. He'd been working at the stable for years and truly loved the horses. Occasionally he'd help at Doc Walters practice if anyone brought an ailing horse in for treatment. Charlie had a way of talking to the horses and soothing their problems.

Sam headed north out of Wichita toward the Flint Hills. Although he'd ridden through the hills before, he wasn't completely familiar with all the small valleys and mountain ranges throughout the area. His goal was to get lost for a few days, clear his mind, and then return to his life.

Sam didn't do much rough-terrain riding so he saw the route would be a challenge for him. Sand mixed with packed earth, with red rock poking through in some areas. Eventually the rock dominated, and the horse's shoes clacked loudly, occasionally throwing sparks. Sam looked ahead and saw more rocks as the hills went higher in elevation. He did see some brush grass sprouting through cracks in the rocks. Somewhere seeds had found water and reached their blades up towards the sun.

Sam was keeping an eye on the terrain where Sweetie was putting her hooves. Some of the rocks were loose; the last thing they needed was a cannon, or pastern bone injury. He wasn't worried for Larry's hoof placement: tethered to Sam's saddle, the big Morgan literally followed in the lead horse's footsteps. While man and horse watched where they stepped, they should have also paid better attention to the sounds around them.

Sweetie saw the rattlesnake seconds before it struck. As she reared up, the snake's strike swung low. Sam was caught unaware and toppled backwards off his saddle, landing hard on the rocks and packed earth. His head struck dirt, not rock, so he was only mildly stunned. As he started to sit up, he thought he heard more rattling off to his right, so he rolled to his left; a mistake. He hit a patch of loose stones and found himself in the middle of a small avalanche. He rolled down the hill ass over teakettle, trying to grab onto anything to halt his fall.

His legs wind-milled, flipping him around. Now tumbling head-first, he saw a large boulder ahead that had his name written all over it. He had no intention of busting his gourd, so he threw his weight to the left which swung him past the boulder, but he hit a hard lump of dirt and caught air. He struck a boulder and was knocked out cold.

"Ow."
Sam held his hand to his head and tried sitting up.
"Ow, fuckit, ow!" Daggers stabbed into his head and neck, and fireworks exploded behind his eyelids. He slowly opened his eyes and saw nothing but nighttime sky, but he heard what sounded like wings. How long was he unconscious? He heard Sweetie whinny, and he looked up to where he thought his horses were.
"Sweetie, Larry, you, okay?" He couldn't see them but heard their shoes scraping the stones. He tried to spin his body around but immediately felt pain shoot through his right knee. He found he couldn't move. The first thing he thought was that he was paralyzed, but then found his right leg was wedged between two large boulders. He could wiggle his toes, but not the leg. In addition, his holstered pistol was wedged and putting pressure on his thigh.
"Goddamnit. Dammit it all to Hell! I hate snakes, I hate them, I –" He realized there might be a rattler still slithering around and knew he was not in any position to defend himself.
"Sweetie, Larry, do you guys see where that snake went?"
Nothing. It's not like he expected them to answer him.
"Do you mean, this snake?" Said a voice from behind him.
Sam's head whipped around. There in front of him stood a naked woman holding a dead snake. It took him a moment to grasp what he was staring at. His mind recognized the snake, but it was the woman he really focused on. She was tall, at least six feet, and she had long golden-brown hair that cascaded over her shoulders and down her back. From his angle on the ground, it looked like she had small feathers woven throughout her hair. He had never seen that before, not even amongst the tribes, but her coloring showed her to be native. She had an oval face, a small nose, full red lips and huge yellow eyes. The irises were black, and her meager eyebrows accented the roundness of

her eyes.

She held the dead snake in a hand with the longest black nails he'd ever seen. Her shoulders were broad, and her breasts large.

"Eyes up here, little man. Did you fall and get yourself stuck?"

"Um, well… "

"What's the matter, bird got your tongue?" Sam turned toward a new voice. A second naked woman, this one sitting on a rock behind him. They weren't twins, but clearly sisters. The new arrival had darker hair, the same eyes and smaller breasts. Her legs were apart and she was giving Sam an eyeful. He was torn between looking away or taking it all in.

"See something you like, little man?" Asked the newcomer.

"I think he'll like me better, sister." Came a third woman's voice. Sam looked down and saw her squatting on a large boulder above his feet. This one was trimmer than the other two, blonde and had a hungry look to her. Her thighs quivered as she squatted on the rock, and her shoulders and triceps flexed as she leaned forward to look at his leg.

"Looks like little man is a bit… stuck," she said, giving Sam an evil smile.

"I don't know who you three are – "

"Four, little man." Sam craned his neck up and behind: a fourth naked woman was sitting on a sand bar, holding up four fingers. This was also a sister, but her hair was jet black with more feathers tangled in it. She wore it hanging down over her face. Even though her eyes were covered, their yellow intensity shone through.

"What the Dickens are you doing here?" Sam asked, doing his best to hide his growing fear

The fourth sister said nothing, just swayed back and forth where she sat.

"We are just five sisters looking for a meal," said a fifth voice.

Sam looked down between his legs. A fifth sister, and the most frightening of them all. Her body resembled the first sister, but she had lighter hair and her eyes were not yellow, but black. They reminded him of the shot he used in his black-powder pistol.

"Well, there's nothing here to eat, dahlin', unless your sister over there wants to share her snake."

"Oh, this snake?" Said the first sister as she ripped it's head off and began to force the body down her throat.

"Holy shit," Sam said quietly. He didn't know what hot mess he'd gotten himself into, but he better think quick, else he ended up as dinner.

The fifth sister walked forward to stand over his body. He was starting to grow aroused by her closeness and nudity, but his mind was screaming, *No you idiot!*

"I don't see anything else to eat... except for you, little man," she said, pointing a nasty clawed finger at him.

Shit.

"He doesn't look big enough to satisfy one of us," said the faceless sister.

"I think she's right," said Sam. "I'm on the short side, and I was kinda sick, so I probably taste like shit."

The sister above him squatted down until she was straddling his hips and reached forward with an abnormally long, black fingernail. She began probing his stomach, his arms and then his chest with that nasty looking nail. Sam thought it looked more like a bird's talon, but that was impossible, *wasn't it?*

"Stop it," Sam said.

But the woman kept on poking at his muscles.

"I said, stop it!" Sam drew his Bowie knife from its scabbard on his left hip and swung it at her. She saw it coming and flicked one of her hands out and knocked the knife into the dark.

"You don't look sick to me. I think you look just fine." She pierced his abdomen with her nail, causing Sam to cry out in pain. She withdrew her nail and Sam saw blood on it. She brought it to her nose, sniffed it, then licked it with a pointed, pink tongue. She closed her eyes and smiled in satisfaction. A shudder of fear shot through Sam's body.

"Is it good, sister?"

"Tell us."

"Oh please, oh please."

The fifth sister looked to her siblings and smiled. "He is tasty, sisters. There is a bitter aftertaste, like he has been somewhere forbidden."

The first sister yelled down to him from her perch. "Where have you been, tasty morsel?"

Sam was starting to panic; he broke out into a sweat and breathing heavy while trying to think of how he was going to get out of this situation. His mother always said, *"Honesty is the Best Policy,"* so Sam thought that would be the route to take.

"Nowhere special – just the Camp of the Dead."

This set the five sisters into a frenzy.

The first sister shouted, "I don't believe him! He heard those words somewhere and is just repeating them!"

The blonde sister poked her head out from behind the boulder she had hidden behind. She looked at Sam with new found fear in her glowing yellow eyes. "I don't believe him either, sister."

The fifth sister stared hard at Sam. "Prove it, little man."

Sam thought about it for a couple beats and replied, "Okay, what do you want to hear? How I beat the Crackling Dead? That I had a friendly chat with Matchitehew? Maybe I can tell you about the huge bonfire I stepped into?"

These words sent the sisters shrieking into the night.

"Was it something I said?" Sam said with a smirk on his face.

"He lies," said one of the hidden sisters.

"Maybe," said another.

Another sister crawled out from behind a boulder, and slowly crept towards him.

"What is your name?"

"I'll tell you mine, if you tell me yours."

"Don't do it, sister," called a sister from the darkness.

"Tell him, tell him so he may know what will befall him."

Sam took that to be the first sister.

"Alright, little man, we are the *Tah-tah-kle'-ah*. You should now quake in fear."

Sam's mouth has gotten him into trouble before and this time was no different.

"The Tittie Tockle? Never heard of you."

The five sisters erupted in anger, screaming and threatening him.

Sam *had* heard of the owl witches of the Yakama tribe, but he wasn't going to admit it.

"Little man, tell us your name!" Came a shrill voice from above. Instead of a lovely naked woman, Sam now saw a giant, fierce owl perched on a boulder. He heard a flutter of heavy wings, as another voice cried at him.

"Tell us your name, or we slice you open and eat your liver!"

He looked to his right and the blonde was gone. In her place was a yellow and brown owl, scraping deep gouges into the boulder with its talons.

"I think I liked you better as a blonde." The third owl threw back its head and screeched in angry frustration.

The fifth sister charged towards him, her body's edges blurring in the air like panicked wings. Her face shifted from that of a beautiful woman to one of an enraged owl. By the time she was atop him, fully morphed, she grasped his throat with a fur-covered four-clawed talon.

She brought her huge face down to his and in a screechy, feminine voice, demanded, "Tell me your name!"

Sam wrinkled his nose, she smelled like three-day old kill. She was choking him, but didn't want to show any weakness. "Sam Hawkins".

"Never heard of you," she replied. He could have sworn she winked at him.

"Some people call me 'Resurrection Sam.'"

A few shrill squawks came from behind the boulders, and he saw the other two sisters resume their places up on high. Both giant owls were clearly upset.

"I know that name," said the blonde owl. "The wind whispers his name. He is the man who dies and is reborn.”

"What good is being reborn after we tear him to shreds?”

Sam was guessing the snake didn't satisfy the owl witch. She clearly wanted to eat him alive. *And I've been so nice to her too*, he thought.

"'Tell me Samhawkins, how you came to be in the Camp of the Dead?” Said the owl in front of him.

"It wasn't hard, I just had to die.”

This started another flurry of screeches and squawks as the five sisters conversed between themselves. The owl in front of him screeched louder than the others. She flapped her brown and gold wings and sprang into the air, momentarily disappearing in the night sky. She reappeared on one of the large boulders trapping his leg.

"Enough!” She yelled into the night.

The other four became silent. At least Sam now knew who the head of the *Tah-tah-kle'-ah* was.

The lead owl sat on the rock and ruffled her feathers. “What should we do, my sisters?”

"Rip him apart!”

"Eat his heart!”

"It will do no good, he will just come back.”

"Then let him come back. We'll eat his liver again!” Screeched the first sister.

A low rumble of thunder interrupted their conversation. This far out in the desert, there was no light, and the moon was only half full. Sam could scarcely any clouds in the sky.

"Enough, sisters!” Screeched the leader of the owl witches. The night sky answered her with another thunderclap.

"We will make a decision before the storm comes.”

Sam's mouth opened and the usual shit came out of it. “I can wait. You just go on squabblin.’”

"Shut up, Samhawkins!” Yelled the snake-eater as she leapt straight up, unfurled her wings and dropped down on his chest. If this was a normal owl, Sam wouldn't have minded, but she was five feet tall and weighed two hundred pounds. He didn't feel like she broke any ribs, but he didn't want her jumping on him again, anytime soon.

"Shut up, Samhawkins!" She screamed again and began striking him across the face with one of her talons.

"Sister, stop!" Yelled one of the other owl witches, as a flash of lightning lit up the mountainside.

It seemed Sam's mouth had finally worn thin on the witch, because she kept ranting and raving for him to be quiet. She listed which of his organs she was going to eat. As storm clouds billowed closer and closer, more thunder and lightning accentuated the scene.

The owl witch stopped beating him, instead she raised a foot into the air, its four razor sharp claws aimed at Sam's face. Suddenly thunder struck so loudly that Sam reasoned this was the center of the storm. A blaze of lightning circled the landscape, seeking a place to light.

Before the harpy could strike, something flashed through her at incredible speed, decapitating her. Her headless body jerked, then toppled backwards into the dirt. Blood poured from her neck-hole like an oil strike.

"Sister!" Two of the owl witches screamed in unison.

"What did Samhawkins do?"

"Sam Hawkins didn't do shit," said Sam, a tinge of desperation in his voice.

He lay in the dirt covered with owl blood, wondering what happened, when thunder struck again, and there was another flash of lightning. The blonde owl exploded in a shower of blood, gore, organs and feathers.

"Sisters!" Screamed one of the owl harpies.

Thunderclaps boomed and echoed, flashes of lightning rippled and crackled, and the sharp taint of blood filled the air. The three remaining owls were petrified. A flash of lightning revealed enormous claws suddenly lighting upon the shoulders of the faceless owl pinning her wings to her side. Sam saw the silhouette of a gigantic raptor behind her with blazing gold eyes that tracked lightning as they moved. Great torrents of blood sprayed into the air as her body was ripped apart. Feathers filled the night air. The two halves of her body plopped onto the dry desert floor, meat for the nights many scavengers. The second owl, perched above Sam's right side, screeched in horror, yelling for its older sister to save them.

"What do we do? What is this terrible thing that has killed our sisters?"

The older owl had taken refuge behind the large rocks that pinned Sam. She hunkered down as low as she could. Her head and eyes jerked in every direction, trying to get a bead on what was attacking them.

"My sister," said the old owl, "Take shelter, whatever is out there will leave if we are not a threat."

Sam rather doubted that logic. Pinned as he was, there was nothing he could do than to suppress his terror. He hoped for his own chance to see whatever was out there.

"Sister, did you hear me?"

Both Sam and the owl witch looked to where the sister had been perched, just as a flash of lightning showed nothing but dripping blood and loose feathers being whipped away by the wind.

"Sisters!" Screeched the last of the owl witches.

In response, thunder rumbled and boomed across the sky so loudly that Sam had to clap his hands over his ears. He could faintly hear his horses scream out in terror as they sought a safe place to hide. Sam felt helpless. Sam *was* helpless. He loved his horses more than he did most people, and he feared they would lash out against the storm and hurt themselves. He tried yelling their names, but the storm drowned out his voice. Lightning flashes lit the desert in yellow and gold, painted the sky in brilliant purple and blues. Bolts of blazing white sizzled both landscape and retina with blinding fury.

The thunder and lightning grew in intensity. Sam felt himself being overwhelmed and on the verge of blacking out. He saw the last *Tah-tah-kle'-ah* looking up into the sky with wide eyes and an open mouth most likely screaming for its life. The thunder rang out louder and louder while the lightning strikes flashed so often that the sky looked like it was raining light. Deafened, seemingly on the verge of madness, Sam finally rolled to his side as far as he could, screamed into the night, and passed out.

When Sam opened his eyes, he saw light blue sky with a scattering of white cumulus clouds. He heard a gentle breeze whispering up from the plains, bringing with it the scent of cudweed and sand verbena. As he lay in the dirt, Sam remembered the night before when the owl witches of the Yakama tribe tortured him. His trapped leg was still good and stuck. He arched his head back, looking for his horses, but couldn't see them.

"Sweetie! Larry! Where are you?"

No response. Nothing but a strange clucking sound coming from the other side of the clearing. Perched on a boulder sat a golden - brown eagle of imposing height. Perhaps as tall as six feet high. Its blazing golden eyes looked over at Sam and clucked again. It raised a foot and began nibbling at something caught between its talons. Sam gasped when he saw the large bird was eating a tiny, incapacitated owl. He could swear he heard the small bird pleading for mercy.

The eagle spread out its white-tipped wings and began preening. When the bird bowed its head down, Sam saw a pair of small, twisted horns, sweeping back along its broad skull. When it looked back at him, a flash of lightning crossed its eyes.

"Hello, Samhawkins."

"H – hi?"

"Do not worry, Samhawkins, I will not hurt you. We are brothers and you are under my protection."

"But – who the hell are ya?"

The bird threw its head back in a raspy laugh. "I am *Animikii*. Your people call me the Thunderbird."

"That was you last night, with the owls."

Another, screeching laugh. "*The Tah-tah-kle'-ah*, are no more, they were the last five."

"I appreciate you saving my life, but why?"

The Thunderbird looked at him, cocked its head and ruffled its wings. "Rolling Thunder asked me to protect you. I could not deny my brother's request."

"Rolling Thunder –?" Sam remembered the old shaman with the wood eagle mask that oversaw his cleansing ceremony. He touched his chest and could almost feel the red paint that bore the shape of the thunderbird.

"*Meegwetch*, thank you, great flying spirit."

The Thunderbird cackled. "You do know some things of the tribes. That is good, because you will need to know more, before you can finally rest."

That didn't fill Sam with encouragement. The bird made it sound like Sam would live longer than he wanted too.

"I don't suppose you could help me out of this?" He said, gesturing to the two boulders. The Thunderbird glared at him as if the effort was an indignity to the great bird. "Aah, here they are," said the bird.

Sam looked and saw Sweetie and Larry walking his way. They must have made it down the hill and found a safe place during the previous night's storm.

"Hey!" Sam yelled out, smiling. Both horses hurried along, swinging their tails with excited energy.

Sweetie worked her way around the boulders and stood over him, while Larry was pondering the boulders.

The Thunderbird made a clicking noise with its beak while looking at Larry.

"*Tonka pejòshkwe.*"

Larry nodded his shaggy head and spun away from the boulders. Looking over a shoulder to set his sights, he began kicking at the boulders with his hind hooves.

"Holey shit, Larry, you're going to hurt yourself."

"Have faith, Samhawkins," said the Thunderbird.

Bits of rock and a cloud of dust rose into the air as Larry continued to kick. Cracks slowly formed on the boulder and soon shards of rock began to break away. The Morgan's rear hooves continued to slam into the rock until there was a final loud crack, and the rock splintered and fell away. Sam freed himself, and flexed his knee, bringing circulation and feeling back to his leg.

"Great job, Larry!" The packhorse nodded his head and flapped his lips.

Sweetie had stood over Sam to protect him from any flying pieces of rock. She made sure he knew it by nickering at him.

"And thank you, Sweetie." He reached up and grabbed the saddle fender as she backed away. He pulled himself up. Once he was standing, he patted Sweetie's broad head and kissed her muzzle. Larry made some silly noises and pawed at the ground.

"I think someone deserves some apples and carrots," said Sam.

"By the way, *Animikii,* –" Sam said as he turned, but the Thunderbird had left without a sound: no thunder, no lightning, just a single two-foot gold and white feather that Sam tucked away in his saddlebag. He rode away from the hills and headed south, towards Wichita.

He looked to the sky, hoping he would see *Animikii* flying overhead, but the great bird was long gone.

No matter where he went, Sam was *now* convinced the weird stuff would follow him forever.

After everything Sam had been through, he deserved a peaceful ride into the hills with his horses. Of course that's not how the story turned out. The nugget of idea I had, was a friendly chat between Sam and the Thunderbird. But it had no tension or intrigue. I feared that it'd be a boring idea.

Then I remembered Mike Mignola introducing readers to the Bird Women of Thessaly, so I searched through materials on American Native creatures and found the owl witches. They were the perfect "villains" I needed for the story and I got to play around with five different personalities, and overlapping voices. It was a challenge but also a lot of fun.

Sam does eventually have his chat with the Thunderbird, and we get to see packhorse Larry, in action.

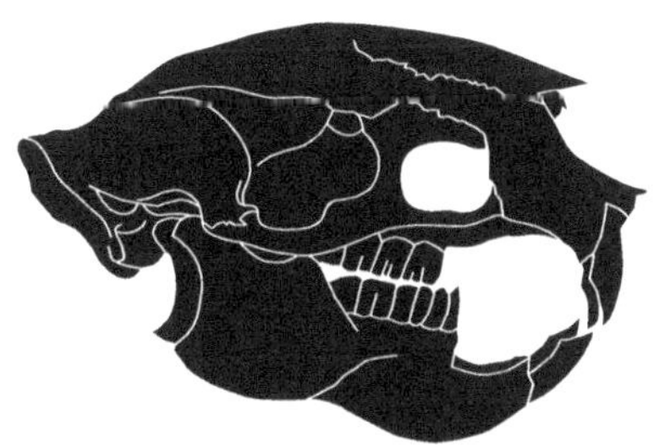

Pukwudgies

"For Pete's Sake, Two Trees cut the bullshit."

"Watch your language, little brother."

"Little brother" was an endearing name the giant Black/Native had for Sam Hawkins. Two Trees stood seven feet tall and weighed over three hundred and fifty pounds, all muscle. Sam Hawkins, stood five-feet-five inches and topped the scales at one hundred and fifty pounds, on a good day. They made an odd team, but they liked each other and worked well together.

But today, Sam was getting on Two Trees' ass about making bank and paying off his indentured servant contract with the owners of the Pretty Kitty. He was a few hundred dollars short and Sam, who always had decent paying jobs come his way, wanted to help his friend.

"Listen, *Wequanunk*, this is your chance to buy out your contract and be your own man. Don't you think that would make Aponi happy?"

Two Trees disliked the nickname. He had never been a stump, but he knew what Sam was trying to do, urging him to be his own man. He had grown up as a slave in Florida. He was sold into indentured slavery due to his giant stature and enormous penis. The Pretty Kitty was the largest and most diverse whorehouse in the territory and always prided itself on having what everyone wanted. Two Trees was their "extreme exotic," a big money maker for the club.

"We know it would make my wife happy, but this move makes me nervous."

Sam said, "I see it as a simple business deal. They have a contract; it has a payout fee. You go with me on this job, you get the entire pay. You pay them, and then you are a free man. No more oiling up your big muscles and bedding those smelly, old rich women who can afford your services."

Two Trees stood up from the small kitchen table in the shack he shared with his wife, Aponi. He went to the teapot and topped off his clay mug. He gestured to Sam for more tea, but the small man shook his head.

Two Trees leaned against the counter. "I don't want to take your money, Sam. I will save up what I need on my own."

"And how long will that take? I'm doing okay for money, and I want you to take this."

"Well... "

"Think about it. The job is escorting a new cook for the mining company. We ride up, we ride back, and we get paid. It's that simple."

"As simple as the last time we worked together?"

"That was just a one-time thing. Who could have guessed we would run into a vampire clan?"

"*I* certainly did not," said Two Trees.

Sam ignored the sarcasm. "We got paid, didn't we?"

"You were killed, Sam. Bitten by a vampire."

"Yeah, but we found out my blood kills vampires. I see that as a positive."

"You were killed, Sam."

"You got paid, right?"

"Yes."

"Well –"

"And I fucked the nurse."

Sam stood up knocking over his tea and pointed at his friend. "I knew it. Dammit, I knew it!" He turned and walked away in frustration.

"It was at work, Sam. She paid for it."

"It doesn't matter, you beat me to it."

"She left town, so it doesn't matter anymore," said Two Trees.

Sam walked back, picked up his mug and started wiping up the mess he made.

"So, are you coming?" Asked Sam.

"No risk, just out and back?"

"Out and back, a big paycheck and your freedom."

"Okay, I am in," said Two Trees with a sigh, looking down into his tea mug.

Sam came over to him and gripped the giant's massive shoulders.

"That's fantastic, you won't regret it."

If Two Trees only knew what those words would eventually mean.

Sam met Two Trees at the Wichita Livery where they were introduced to the new cook for the Wichita Mining Company.

"Good morning, I'm Rhys Macgillicuddy. I assume you are Sam and Two Trees?"

"Rhys?" Asked Sam.

"Yes."

"R-e-e-s-e?"

"No, R-h-y-s."

"Well, I'm going to call you Mac, how does that sound?" Said Sam.

Two Trees held out his frying pan-sized hand and the cook shook it. "Do not mind him, he has a boring name like "Sam". He does not let people forget it."

"Damn, you are a big one. I feel safe already."

Sam stepped between the two men and took Rhys' hand in his.

"Don't you worry, we'll make sure you're safe all the way to the mining camp."

Macgillicuddy was of average height and stocky, with a big mess of red hair and a red beard that looked more like a bird's nest. His chuck wagon was behind the livery stable. While Sam and Two Trees saddled their horses, Mac brought his wagon around to the front of the stables.

The two men walked their horses from the stable; Sam had Sweetie ready to go, while Two Trees' horse was huge. It also had to be one of the ugliest horses Sam had ever seen. Its eyes were offset, its mane was scraggly, and the horse's tail was more flesh and bone than it was hair.

Two Trees said the horse was an Appaloosa, but Sam had his own thoughts on the animal's breeding history. It concerned a jackass, a buffalo and a gopher. He kept that to himself.

"*Kitchi*, don't listen to him. He is just jealous."

"As long as your "Brave" can make the trip, I will keep my mouth shut."

Mac sat on the driver's bench and shook his head. "You two are like an old married couple."

Two Trees looked at the Irishman. "Sometimes."

Mac's chuck wagon was a covered wagon pulled by two Morgans, one white and one brown. It had extra barrels lashed to the sides, and bags of beans, rice, coffee, sugar and corn sitting on top of the wooden cases inside the wagon. The rear of the wagon could be lowered and used as a worktable. Inside were storage cubbies as well as drawers full of other dried foods and seasonings. At least the three of them would eat well on the two-day trip to Osage County and the coal mines.

"Mac; Two Trees and I will take the lead and set the pace. We shouldn't have any Indian problems, so just keep an eye out for coyotes and buffalo." Said Sam.

"Alrighty, I've got your backs. We see any buffalo try and take one down. It would be great to roll into camp with some fresh meat."

Sam nodded at Mac. They turned their horses and road out of town, headed north. Two Trees was nervous riding away from the safety of the town and his wife. The night before, she was torn on the option of paying off his contract or continuing their life as it was. In the end, she wanted her man to herself and thought the risk was worth it. Two

Trees made sure he had extra ammunition for his '76 Winchester, and had a Colt single action revolver tucked away in his saddlebag. He wasn't a fan of revolvers, but decided the extra firepower would come in handy in case of trouble. He had a tomahawk tucked into his leather belt and a war club sheathed behind his saddle. Two Trees was shit at using a bow, so he didn't bother packing one.

Sam had his trusty LeMat pistol, with extra shot and powder in his saddlebag. After losing his .73 Winchester in the vampire fiasco, he'd picked up a used Sharp's rifle. It was a single shot weapon but was great at long distances and would be perfect for bagging the buffalo Mac wanted. Sam carried a Bowie knife on his hip and had replaced his throwing knife, he kept in a hidden sheath in his vest. At least he was fully armed and ready for any mischief that would come their way.

It was unknown what weapons Mac had tucked away in the chuck wagon, but Sam guessed at least a few knives and cleavers. Being a travelling cook that roamed the plains, meant you were a tough bastard and could handle yourself. Sam figured the Irishman would be good help in a fight.

Their first day on the road was uneventful. The best thing that happened was Sam shot and killed a bull buffalo for Mac's menu once they arrived at the mining camp. Besides that, all was quiet. They ate some tasty meals and slept soundly. At one point, Kitchi decided he wanted to get amorous with Sweetie, but she quickly shut that down with a bloody bite to his ear. Two Trees cleaned the wound and had a heart-to-heart talk with his horse. Sam thought it was one of the funniest things he had ever heard.

The second morning, Sam offered to make some of his famous Johnny cakes as Mac worked on a quick marmalade using prickly pear cactus. Along with some strong coffee, the three men ate their fill, and then packed up for the last leg of the trip.

As they rode northward, Sam turned to Two Trees. "So far, so good."

"I have to admit, *nomattimen*, you were right – so far."

"It's a beautiful day, our bellies are full, and I see no troubles ahead of us."

"Speaking of ahead of us!" Mac yelled from behind them. They turned around and saw him pointing off to the distance. As they swung around to see what he was pointing at, both of their hearts skipped a beat. Ahead of them in the far distance was a large veil of dense, black smoke.

"Oh shit."

Even at this distance they began to smell the smoke. This fire had been burning for some time.

Two Trees stood up in his saddle and took in deep breaths of the smoke.

"I smell wood smoke, mixed with coal. I also smell what might be cooked meat."

Sam looked over his shoulder at Mac. "What do you think?"

"It doesn't look good." Rhys Macgillicuddy, a man of few words.

Sam asked, "Can you get any speed out of your team?"

Mac nodded his head, "We've been chased by the best and are still breathin'. We'll keep up."

Sam drew his Sharps rifle from its saddle sheath. Two Trees was already cocking his Winchester.

Sam looked at his friend. "Sorry."

Two Trees shrugged his shoulders.

"Let's go!" Sam yelled as he raised his rifle in the air. They spurred their horses into a run. Behind them they heard, "Sugar, Coffee, heey-aw!"

Both riders smirked when they heard the horses' names.

They rode hard to cover the miles to the mining camp. Mac managed to keep up, only lagging by a half-mile. It probably was for the best the riders were heavily armed and ready to shoot anything out of the ordinary.

As Sam and Two Trees rode into camp, they saw the buildings on fire and sooty smoke coming from the coal mine's opening. Worse, there were a few burned corpses scattered around the camp.

They pulled up and tied their horses to a hitching post in front of the manager's office. It too had been set on fire, but had burnt out already, leaving half the structure standing. As the two men realized the scope the tragic scene around them, Mac drove his wagon into camp. Sam waved him to put the horses and wagon near theirs and away from the burning fires.

Mac ran over to them carrying his own Winchester rifle.

"What's the plan?"

Sam looked around. "We sweep along the rise and check out any buildings that are on fire. If we find anyone alive, we get them to your wagon."

The other men nodded in agreement and started a careful investigation of the ridge. This Wichita mining camp was established four years earlier and was a split-level dig. The office, barns, dining tent and bunkhouses all surrounded a pit that led down to the mine. A well-worn road led from the top down to the mine entrance.

Strewn along the ground leading to the mine were more burned bodies, pickaxes, shovels, and a few upturned coal cars. A few yards before the entrance, the coal car tracks led into the mine. Somewhere, Sam reckoned, was a stable with at least a dozen mules that were used to pull the carts in and out of the mine.

The three men began a sweep of the buildings, starting with the manager's office. Inside was pure disorder. Broken furniture and loose papers were strewn about the room.

"Nothing here. Let's search the rest of the buildings and then meet back here. Go through this mess more thoroughly," said Sam.

"Sounds good," said Mac.

"Be careful," said Two Trees.

Sam looked at his friend and raised his eyebrows in a questioning look.

Two Trees shook him off as they continued looking for survivors and clues that would tell them what had happened here.

They found the telegraph room had suffered a lot of damage. Whoever had destroyed the equipment had crushed it into small pieces. There would be no repairing it.

The dining tent was still on fire, and a quick look showed a few burned corpses.

"Mac, how many people worked here?" Asked Two Trees.

The Irishman looked up at the giant and said, "An operation this size would have around thirty-five men and probably a dozen mules."

"Mules are pretty darn loud, I don't hear anything," said Sam.

The three men paused for a second. The only sound was that of the wind coming over the plains and the crackling of scattered fires.

"Let's check out the bunkhouses and then go over to the barn and look for any mules."

Both bunkhouses were fully engulfed in flames and smoke. The men peeked inside as best as they could. If anyone was left inside, they were likely dead.

"What the hell happened here?" Asked Mac.

"I have no idea," said Sam.

"To the barn," said Two Trees.

The men worked their way to the other side of the pit where the barn was located. It was used for housing small animals and storing lumber and other building supplies. There were no signs of life inside. No dead men or animals. There was lumber and tools strewn around but nothing looked to be obviously missing.

"Where the feckin' hell is everybody!" Yelled Mac as he turned around and took in the entire site.

Two Trees whispered to Sam, "Can I speak to you in private?" Sam gave him a nod and they stepped a few yards away from Macgillicuddy as the cook continued to wander the camp.

Sam looked up at his friend. "I know what you are going to say."

"No. That *is* what I am saying. We did our job. He is here," gesturing to Mac. "It is time to leave."

"I know that's what we signed on for, but –"

"No buts."

"But... " Sam said to his friend, "There are people both missing and dead, I can't believe you could walk away from them."

Two Trees frowned because he partially agreed with Sam. He had a big heart, but he also had no intention of tussling with vampires, shape changers, skinwalkers or Windigo.

"I will agree to search the camp a bit more, but then we pack up Macgillicuddy and leave."

"What about the mine?"

"I am not going in there," said Two Trees.

"If something bad has happened to these miners, the mine is the obvious place to search."

Mac walked over to them after watching their exchange.

"Is there something I should know?"

The two men turned to face the cook but neither of them knew quite what to say.

"We were just discussing what to do. We signed on to escort you, but we can't turn around and leave you here," Sam said.

Two Trees added, "Do you want to leave?"

"I'm not sure," Mac said. "I didn't know anyone at this camp, but I can't go back to the mining company and tell them everyone is dead without giving them some answers."

They decided to go back to the manager's office, and sort through the mess of papers. Maybe they could find something that would give them some insight. Depending upon what they found, they might leave and head back to Wichita.

Inside the office, the men spent time looking through wooden filing cabinets and the manager's desk. Sam came across something of interest. He decided to share it with the others.

"Fellas, if I may?" He said as he raised the manager's daily log. The two others nodded and Sam began:

"*Daily Work Reports – Jerome Sullivan, manager.*

Seventeen, August 1875. Mining has gone well. More clean coal coming out of tunnel Twelve, while tunnels Eight and Ten stay consistent. Men on the overnight watch have complained of hearing weird noises. I made sure they were armed. These are tough miners and almost nothing scares them.

"*Nineteen, August 1875. There were more complaints from the men about strange noises at night. Day shift broke through the bottom of tunnel Twelve and found a series of shafts.*

Samples taken showed the tunnels are lined with coal like never seen before! Second shift began shoring up the new tunnels with lumber.

We will begin digging once we know the tunnels are safe."

Sam looked away from the journal to his companions. "Thoughts?"

"Sounds like they had good luck and were making money," said Mac.

Sam looked at his Indian brother. "Trees?"

"Greed wins over common sense." Sam nodded his head and read on.

"*Twenty-one, August 1875. The new tunnel is delivering beautiful coal. Third shift reports three men have not shown up for work. Their belongings are still in the bunkhouse.*

"Twenty-two, August 1875. Six men have not reported for work on third shift. Only two men worked. They did the best they could. I will move them to second shift. Reports of whispering heard down tunnel A.

"Twenty-three, August 1875. Second shift came up from tunnel Twelve A, missing six men. The supervisor had seen them before coming up, but not above ground. Messages have been sent out to the home office through telegraph, but we have not received any responses."

Sam stopped for a second. "We saw the telegraph room busted up, but he doesn't mention it here. Maybe wires somewhere along the way came down during a windstorm?"

"I was in too much of a hurry to get here to notice," said Mac.

Sam cleared his throat before continuing.

"Twenty-five, August 1875. Production in the mine has stopped. There are only eight of us left and no one wants to go into the mine. Everyone claims to hear whispers and noises at night.

No one goes out until sunrise. All the mules have disappeared.

The stable gate as left open, and their hoof prints were tracked going into the mine.

All the chickens are gone. We found a few of them torn apart, with feathers and blood all over the floor of the barn.

We are hoping the new cook has room for all of us in his wagon. As soon as he gets here, we are going to return to Wichita.

Everyone is afraid."

"Shite. I was to be their rescue," said Mac.

"Twenty-six, August 1875. Four more men disappeared last night. It was said they were talking to someone and then left the bunk-house. The telegraph room was broken into, and all the equipment was destroyed.

There is no chance of repairing it.

"Twenty-seven, August 1875. I checked on the other three men and their bunks had been slept in, but I could not find them anywhere in camp.

I am the only one left. I've been sleeping in my office. Heard shuffling outside my door and scraping on the walls. I am very afraid.

I hope to see the sun rise in the morning."

"That's it", said Sam.

"No more entries?" Asked Mac.

"Take a look for yourself," said Sam, passing the logbook over to the cook.

Mac flipped through the written pages and then jumped all the way to the end. He found nothing after the twenty-seventh. Two Trees had leaned over and looked at the pages along with Mac. The big man had a scowl on his face. To anyone but Sam, that look said to get out of the giant's way because something bad was about to happen. To Sam, it meant that Two Trees had finally concluded that something had to be done to right the wrong dealt to the miners of this camp.

Two Trees made a grunting noise deep down in his throat. Mac looked up at him in fear. Not only was the sound terrifying, but the look on the giant's face would have scared the Devil.

Two Trees walked to the office door, kicked it open and stalked away from the building. Sam and Mac looked at each other, and Sam shrugged his shoulders in answer to Mac's silent question. Sam ran after Two Trees. Mac followed, unsure of what was going on.

"Where are we going?" Asked Mac.

"I don't know," said Sam.

"Umm, where is he going?" Mac pointed in Two Trees' direction.

"Looks like the mine."

"Why?"

"Why do you think?" Sam asked, looking back at the cook.

"I thought we were leaving?"

"Looks like things have changed."

"Shit."

Two Trees' long legs carried him away from the other men, up to the long dirt ramp that led toward the mine. As he got closer, he began to search the ground for any signs of the miners.

He looked over his shoulder at the cook and asked, "Were there any children here?"

"Children? No. All men. No women or children per company's rules, why?"

The giant had dropped down into a crouch to more closely examine the soil. He waved his fingers over some tracks and felt how firm the dirt was. "There are boot marks from the miners, leading there." He pointed to the mine entrance.

"At least we know where they went," said Sam.

"Yes... but there are small footprints mixed in with those of the miners."

"Maybe some of the men had small feet?" Asked Mac.

"These footprints are bare."

"No shit," said Sam.

"That can't be right," said Mac.

Two Trees stood up and stared at the cook. "Are you saying I don't know how to track?"

Mac realized he had just crossed a line and put up his hands in submission. "No, I, I mean, it's just crazy. There shouldn't be any children here."

"I know what the earth tells me."

"Okay, now that we've established that Two Trees is a fantastic tracker, what are we going to do?" Asked Sam.

Two Trees turned and started toward the mine entrance at a quick pace.

Sam lurched forward, trying to keep up with his friend.

Mac jogged alongside Sam. "What are we doing?"

Sam looked over at the Irishman. "Looks like we're going into the mine."

'Shit," said Mac.

Ke'eeps.

"What did he say?" Asked Mac.

"I think he cooks *chickens*. I don't think he is one."

Upon reaching the mine entrance, the three stopped to look in. The light of the midday sun penetrated twenty feet before the dark ate it up. It would eat more as the Earth spun eastward.

Two Trees looked up at the sun and back at the mine. "If we are going in, now is the time. We will lose the sun in two hours, once it drops below the ridge."

Two Trees started into the mine when Sam jumped in front of him and put his hand on the giant's chest.

"Hold on, brother. I'm the impulsive one. We need to kit up before we go inside."

"What do we need?" Asked Two Trees.

Sam looked around and spotted something he knew was necessary. He picked up two canvas mining caps with oil-wick lamps. "We need these if we want to see down there."

"And?"

Sam looked around again and picked up a shovel and a pickaxe. He held them up before his friend, and Two Trees nodded.

Mac came over holding three Mueseler lamps. "We're going to need these. Those cap lamps aren't good for shit."

"And what about the caps?" Asked Two Trees.

"They're fine if you have a hard head."

Sam asked, "So they'll just get in the way?"

"Yeah," said Mac.

Sam looked up at his brother. "Now we're ready."

They scanned the entrance to the mine; nothing seemed out of sorts. Nor did it look like Dante's entrance to Hell, with its warning sign that read "Abandon all hope, ye who enter here." The opening was rectangular and framed by heavy timbers. The top of the entrance had additional timbers stacked for support and a small wall of rectangular stones above that. Shovels, picks and loose timbers were strewn around the sides of the pit.

The three men lit their lamps from wood matches Mac had in his pocket. Two Trees took the lead with Sam taking the rear, they stepped into the inky darkness.

They descended into a world of soot, dust, low-hanging smoke and just enough light to let them see before they lost their footing.

For once, Sam was glad of his lack of height. He could stand perfectly upright and not worry about banging his head. Two Trees, on the other hand, was bent at an awkward angle. When he forgot where he was, he'd hit his head on a cross beam or a low hanging chunk of rock. He would grunt and rub his head, but never swear. Mac could almost stand straight up, but occasionally Sam would hear *"Feckin' bullocks,"* *"goddamn bowsie,"* *"stupid coppernob,"* and *"I must ha' been an eejit."* Sam thought the last phrase was his favorite.

As they walked down the long tunnel, they saw the presence of the miners – Discarded mining caps, shovels, picks, a torn shirt – but no bodies. The air was so thick with the smell of dirt and coal that nothing else was discernible. Before long Sam noticed scratches along the walls that were belt high. He couldn't identify what made them. His initial thought were the mining cars. There were chunks of coal scattered along the car rails, but for the most part, it was a well-kept tunnel. They had travelled fifty yards when they found the branch for tunnel Twelve A. The opening had been shored up with rough-hewn timbers.

"Sam, the tracks go down here," said Two Trees as he gestured into Twelve A.

Sam stepped up to his friend and raised his lantern. The tunnel had been supported with heavy timbers and the sides were covered with coal. "Now I see why they wanted to dig here."

"Fellas, do you smell that?" Asked Mac.

"Now that you mention it, I do. I thought it was Sam," said Two Trees with a smirk on his face.

Sam looked at his friend with surprise on his face. "Now is the time you decide to crack a joke? Step aside funny man, I'll take the lead." Sam shouldered his way past the giant, (which barely moved him). He raised his lantern high and proceeded down the tunnel. Sam was grateful that nothing was out of the ordinary, besides being hundreds of feet underground looking for missing miners.

"How does it look up there?" Asked Mac.

"I still don't see any –" Sam came to a hard stop and stood rigid as the other men joined him.

"What is it, Sam?" Asked Two Trees.

"There." Sam said raising his lamp higher so the others could see.

They had entered a small cavern, and it was literally dripping in blood. The floor, walls and ceiling were coated in blood so thick you couldn't see the coal beneath it. The floor itself was like a small lake and a river flowing down the tunnel's incline. A river of blood.

"Holy shite," said the Irishman, as he peered over Sam's shoulder.

"How much blood is in there?"

Sam looked over his shoulder at his friend. "At least thirty-five men's worth."

The other two considered that statement, mulling it over to know good end.

"What the hell happened in there?" Asked Mac.

Two Trees said, "I think it is obvious."

Sam saw a tunnel opening on the other side of the chamber and pointed in its direction. "That's where we need to go."

"You've got to be shittin' me," said Mac as he stepped in front of Sam. Two Trees held back, but if Mac showed any aggression towards his friend, he would step in.

"We came down here to find the miners. I don't see them here, so we move on." Said Sam as he eyeballed the Irishman.

"Feck that! I say we leg it outta here and head back to Wichita."

"And if we don't have any answers on what happened here, another team will come out. Those men could end up dead as well. Is that what you want?" Asked Sam.

Mac lost all his bravado and began examining his leather boots.

"No, feck it."

"Then we move on. Trees, keep an eye on our asses."

The giant nodded as Sam walked past Mac. They did their best to avoid the deeper pools of drying blood, but it just couldn't be helped. If they got back alive from this, they'd all be buying new boots. They made it through the blood chamber and into the next tunnel. They still saw no other living souls. In this tunnel, Sam had to stoop a little.

Mac had his neck bowed with his chin on his chest. Trees was bent in half until he found it easier to crab walk through the tunnel.

They noticed this tunnel was created using a cruder method. The first tunnels were dug using shovels and picks and supported by timbers. The new tunnel was rougher hewn and smaller than the first ones. Sam thought it looked like it had been dug by hand, impossible as that was. After fifty yards into the tunnel, they came across discarded leather boots, shoes, trousers, other pieces of clothing and extinguished lamps.

"Well, shit," said Sam.

Mac came up on his left and saw the clothing. "I guess we found the miners."

Two Trees joined them and looked sadly at the clothing. Sam glanced at him and could read the look on his friend's face. Earlier Trees wanted to get on his horse, ride back to Wichita and collect his money. Now his face said he wanted to collect vengeance.

The three men had started to go further down the smaller tunnel when they heard animalistic hoots up ahead.

All three froze in their tracks.

"What the fuck was that?" Whispered Sam.

Mac came up from behind and pointed past him.

"What the feck is that?"

Six yards ahead, small, shadowy figures crawled towards the men. Their bodies were hairy with long spikes or quills jutting from their back and shoulders. Their eyes reflected yellow by the lamp light. The one in the lead reared back on its haunches and hooted. The sound echoed hauntingly throughout the tunnel. As if in answer, the pack hooted, screamed and became agitated. Sam cocked his pistol and aimed it at the group. Two Trees and Mac raised their rifles and began to target individuals. As soon as the creatures saw the weapons, they stopped and began to slink away back down the tunnel.

Sam began to inch forward. "Be careful," said Two Trees.

"They've seen guns before and know what they can do."

"What does that mean?" Asked Mac.

"It means they're smart."

"Those things? They're just animals," cried Mac.

"A smart animal is a very dangerous thing." Two Trees squeezed by Mac in the cramped tunnel and joined Sam.

"Any idea what they are?" He asked.

"I was going to ask you the same thing," said Sam.

"Aponi mentioned something years ago about a tribe of small creatures with porcupine quills. She called them Pukwudgie."

"At least they're not Windigos," said Sam, jokingly.

Two Trees made no comment. That worried Sam. He looked at his friend with a curious expression on his face. "She said… they are cannibals."

"*Shit,* I didn't need to know that."

"What are you talking about?" Asked Mac.

Sam looked back at him. "Just talking about what we're going to do."

"I say we charge ahead and wipe them out."

"I would not recommend that," said Two Trees.

Mac looked up at the giant, "The devil mends you! There's what, six of them? We'd wipe them out in no time."

"We have no idea how many are sneaking around ahead of us," said Sam.

"Friend, we've got guns and fire. I see no problem charging forward."

Sam looked at his companions. "We could go further in and look around."

"Sam!"

"I know what you're going to say, Trees, but we've got missing men. I need to know if these Pudwugs are responsible."

"Pukwudgies."

"Whatever the fuck they are. Let's go a little further, and if things look rotten, we'll leave."

"Agreed."

"Feckin' right!" Cried Mac.

The three men started forward with Sam still in the lead. They didn't get more than twenty feet, when the hooting resumed. Each man raised their lamps higher looking for the origin of the sounds, but no creatures were seen, so they continued.

Sam's heart was hammering and sweat was running down his face. He didn't like enclosed spaces and the tunnels walls were starting to get under his skin. He imagined the other men, crouched over, weren't having a grand time of it either. And then it happened. The worst misstep of Sam's life. He stepped directly into a small pool of blood. Slippery blood. Very slippery blood. Sam's foot came down, slid forward, throwing off his balance. Both feet now surfing on the near-frictionless blood. He stumbled, cart wheeled, went airborne, and then crashed down upon the tunnel floor with such force, he punched a hole right through it. He dropped down into a void.

"Sam!" Cried Two Trees as he charged with his lamp in front of him, just in case any of the creatures took advantage of the situation.

"Sam, are you alright?"
After a few tense and quiet moments, a reply came from below.
"What the fuck?"
By his response, Two Trees guessed his friend was all right. Mac joined him at the ragged hole, lowering his lamp.
"Hey boyo, can you see this?"
"Barely." Sam had slid down the side of the chamber so only his pride was sore. He was covered with the blood that had weakened the floor of the tunnel. "I think I'm twenty feet below you, I can see the light but not the top of the hole."
"I'm coming down to get you," said Two Trees.
"Forget it, you'll never fit."
The giant looked at the cook. "Not me. I'm not going down there," Mac said as he backed away from the hole.
"*Ke'eeps.*"
"I agree with you this time, *nomattimen,*" came Sam's voice from the void.

Two Trees peered into the hole but couldn't see much besides the irregular sides of the first couple of feet of the hole's walls. "What do you want to do?"

Sam thought about it for a few seconds. "Take Mac and head back to the surface."

"Are you sure?"

"No, but what choice do I have? Those things seem damn good at tunneling, so I'm sure there must be another way out of here."

"Alright, but keep a sharp ear open for any of the Pukwudgies. Aponi said they could be fierce."

Sam looked up into the darkness and took to heart what his friend recommended. Then his mouth opened on its own. "What's the worst they could do, kill me?"

Two Trees didn't laugh at Sam's black humor. "Asshole."

"Whoa, Two Trees Holmes just swore! I'm telling your wife."

He waited for a response, but then realized the lamp glow was gone and he could hear their footsteps fading away.

"Sorry, Trees."

Two Trees and Mac made it out of Twelve A, and into Twelve. As they started to see sun light ahead of them, they heard the hooting of creatures behind them. Two Trees stopped and turned to cover their backs. He could see shapes moving in the shadows, but had no clear targets to shoot at. Mac had turned and called out to him.

"C'mon, Two Trees. We gotta go!"

"Not before I get some revenge."

"Are you crazy?"

"Maybe." The hooting grew louder. Two Trees could see the Pukwudgies were getting closer.

"Stay or go, does not matter to me."

Mac looked at his companion and then glanced towards the front of the tunnel. He had never been so torn in his life. He had just met these men a few days earlier, but for seem reason, they were getting under his skin. He'd grown fond of them.

"Ah feck it!" Said the Irishman, walking back to stand next to the giant native. He raised his rifle and awaited Two Trees' orders. The tunnel ahead began to fill up with the creatures. As soon as they came within twenty feet, Two Trees quietly said, "Now."

The two men fired blindly into the undulating pack charging at them. The creatures began to howl in pain and anger as they saw their brethren being cut down. Their actions became frantic as they threw themselves over the dead bodies of their pack attempting to reach the humans.

The sound of the two Winchesters being fired within the small tunnel was deafening. Gunsmoke filled the tunnel, obstructing the men's vision. The smell of cordite was thick and bitter. The men continued firing and retreating up the tunnel until they ran out of ammunition. A few of the creatures broke through the smoke cloud and charged forward. Both men started swinging their rifles like clubs. Two Trees killed two of the creatures but shattered his rifle's stock into splinters. Mac swung his rifle by the barrel and connected with the face of one creature, and then swung his rifle down onto the head of the next, smashing its face into the rock floor. Two Trees drew his tomahawk and started swinging it from side to side, keeping the little creatures at bay. A head went flying in one direction, a hand and dismembered fingers in another.

The Pukwudgies had never before seen someone like Two Trees Holmes. He fought with the bravery and fierceness of a Windigo. As Two Trees continued to battle the creatures, Mac made his way towards the mine entrance.

"I've reached the main tunnel. Let's go!"

Two Trees risked a glance behind and saw he had forty feet to go before reaching the main tunnel. He looked back and saw that the creatures had halted their attack. They seemed leery of him, as if waiting to see what he was going to do. This gave him a chance to make a quick decision: He turned and ran. A quick sprint and he was in the main tunnel and into the sunshine that lit up the chamber. Several creatures had charged into the chamber only to immediately recoil from the sunlight. They yelped and cried out in pain as their skin beginning to blister and smoke. The sun burned them!

Mac stepped up next to Two Trees and cried out, "Ha! Don't like the sun do ya, ya sorry little shites!"

Two more creatures succumbed to the power of the sun as their bodies burned and smoked on the floor of the chamber. Two Trees took a few steps closer to examine the naked creatures. They were three feet tall, with strong arms. Their three-fingered hands ended in thick, scythe-like black claws. Trees imagined them digging through dirt and rock. The legs were bowed and out of proportion with the torso. Their pizzles were small and hairless, were they all male? The faces reminded him of frogs except for a heavy brow ridge and a well-formed nose. Their eyes were deep set and white, like many cave-dwelling species. The most interesting thing Two Trees discovered about the Pukwudgies were the quills that protruded from the back of their heads, shoulders and backs. Each was a foot in length, dark brown and lay down like a hairy pelt. Two Trees could imagine these being used in close battle, for the ends were barbed and razor sharp.

Mac peered around the giant's shoulder. "Ugly little feckers, aren't they?"

"I've seen worse," said Two Trees. He reached down and tugged on one of the quills. It came out easily. He took care in handling it. Aponi would find it very interesting.

As the creatures in the tunnel hooted and screamed at the two men, some would gingerly step into the sun, only to pull back in pain.

"We need to blow the mine."

"We what?"

"Bring it down on their heads."

"What about Sam?" Asked Mac.

Two Trees looked down on the Irish cook. "If we don't stop these things here and now, the next crew of miners will certainly die."

"But how do we – "

"It is obvious that Twelve A is their home and the miners accidentally broke into it. We need to keep them from ever coming to the surface again."

"And your friend?" Asked Mac.

The giant looked him in the eye. "Sam has a way of getting out of trouble." Then he walked towards the mine entrance with Mac scrambling behind him.

Sam found himself in the dark, alone with the sounds of Pukwudgies scrambling through the earth. Their hoots and cries echoing through the tunnels. He was feeling his way with one hand down a small offshoot tunnel, his oil lamp lost in his fall. In his other hand, his Le Mat pistol held out in front of him. At the first sign of a creature, he'd shoot. He had no intention of becoming dinner for those little bastards.

He shuffled forward. When he felt an opening to his right, he listened for any sounds of movement. He'd take the turn, hoping it would lead to an opening close to the surface.

After twenty yards, Sam stumbled over some objects in the dark. He stopped to feel around for them: a pair of empty work boots... a water canteen... an oil lamp! He searched his vest and pants pockets, and found two loose matches. Sam didn't know if this was dumb luck or cosmic cruelty. He lifted the glass tunnel, struck a match, failed three times before successfully lighting the wick. He lifted the lamp into the air and found himself in a tight tunnel with corpses littering the floor. Some were clothed, some naked. Most were decomposed. The temperature in this tunnel was very cold; he saw his own breath. No steam came from the bodies. Worse, the tunnel ran downhill.

Sam retraced his steps and returned to his previous path. Now armed with the lamp held in front of him, he saw newly dug tunnels opening into the main tunnel. Sand, dirt and broken rocks were piled in front of each opening. He swung his lamp into each, checking to see if any of the creatures were waiting for him. After finding five empty tunnels, Sam felt he was in the clear. He saw one smaller opening to his left, held the lamp up to it and nearly shit his pants.

This was no tunnel but the entrance to a large chamber filled with angry Pukwudgies.

Two Trees and Mac were outside the mine entrance, and heading up its ramp.

"What's the plan?" Asked Mac.

"I'm going to roll dynamite down that tunnel and blow the hell out of it."

"Have you ever used dynamite before?"

The giant stopped in his tracks. "Umm... no."

"Then you're going to need my help."

Two trees looked up at the receding sun. "Time is passing. Let us get to work."

The two men found a few cases of dynamite in the tool shed along with detonation cord and a detonator. They ran back to the mine and wired three bundles of dynamite set to explode simultaneously.

"How far in do you want to place the dynamite?"

Two Trees looked inside the mine and saw that the sun was receding from tunnel Twelve. "As far in as possible."

"Hunh," said Mac, looking into the mine. "Stay here, I'll be right back." He took off running back up the ramp, and headed to the camp.

Two Trees yelled back to him, "If you're running away, I will hunt you down."

"I'll be right back!"

A few too many minutes passed for Two Trees' taste, so he took the three bundles in his arms and started toward the mine entrance.

"Wait!" The cook ran up to him, out of breath with two flat objects tucked under an arm.

"What did you get?"

Mac looked up at Two Trees with a big smile on his face and showed him what he had gone back for: two mirrors from one of the bunkhouses.

Two Trees looked at the mirrors. "Clever. Damn clever."

Holy shit! Sam counted at least forty of the little devils in the chamber. They all just stared at each other until Sam recovered his wits and bolted down the tunnel. The creatures were hot on his heels whooping and hollering with blood on their minds. Sam turned and fired his Le Mat on the run. Eventually his shots ran out. He holstered his gun and continued running as fast as he could, all the while trying to keep his lamp lit. The tunnel turned, twisted and suddenly dropped out of sight. Sam jumped blindly over a dark shadow that may have been a bottomless chasm. He scrambled up the other side as a few of the Pukwudgies leapt but came up short. The creatures tried to gain a hold, but it was a mix of slate and coal and gave no purchase. They slid helplessly down the hole, their cries soon fading to silence. Sam saw the rest of the pack screeching and hooting in frustration. They searched the walls and ceiling for a way across the void. He had no intention of waiting around for them to figure it out. He crested the stone ramp and took off running, cradling his lamp like a newborn child.

"Are you ready?" Cried Mac.

"Almost," came the response from inside the mine. Two Trees carried one of the mirrors into the tunnel, looking for a secure place to set it down. Mac was doing the same thing at the mouth of the tunnel. They hoped to reflect the sunlight far enough down tunnel Twelve to keep the Pukwudgies at bay.

"Ready," said Mac.

Two Trees propped his mirror against a turned-over mining car and angled it toward tunnel Twelve. From inside the tunnel, growing louder each moment, came the sounds of hisses and growls. Mac saw the angle of the Indian's mirror, corrected his, and suddenly tunnel Twelve was bathed in sunlight. Both men heard the screams and cries of the Pukwudgies as they retreated from the blistering light.

"Ha-ha! It works!" Yelled Mac, throwing his arms into the air.

"Well done, Irishman!" Said Two Trees, as he came out of the mine. "Now we show those things how we celebrate!"

Minutes later, Two Trees had placed the first two bundles of dynamite halfway down tunnel Twelve. When he approached the opening to tunnel Twelve A, he stopped and placed the third bundle behind some small boulders.

Two Trees then jogged out of the mine and joined Mac at the top of the ramp.

"Are we good?" Asked Mac.

"Yes."

"Is the sun still shining down the tunnel?"

"Yes."

"Then all we have to do is slam the plunger down and we can go home." Mac walked over to the detonator intending to push the plunger when Two Trees put his pan-sized hand on the man's chest.

"We wait."

"What for?" Mac said with a questioning look on his face.

"For Sam."

"I'm sorry, but he's dead."

"We wait."

"C'mon, he must be dead."

Two Trees looked at Mac. "We. Wait."

Mac saw the look on the giant's face, broke out in a cold sweat and said. "I guess we wait."

Sam was desperate. He hadn't come to the end of the tunnel nor found an exit. He was starting to believe he was fucked. Some of the creatures had found their way across the void and were still chasing him. The hootings and cries continued, nearly pushing Sam beyond his sanity. He came to a stop and held out his lamp to get his bearings. Two small tunnels branched off to his left. He had to decide: stay on the path he was on, or try the two tunnels. He reached into his vest pocket and took out what was left of the golden-brown feather of *Animikii*, the Thunderbird.

Sam rubbed it between his thumb and forefinger, closed his eyes and focused on the feathers owner. He cracked one eye open half-hoping to see bolts of magic lightning amidst roars of thunder, but he found neither. Instead he did see a single ray of light brightening one of the side tunnels. Hearing the screaming creatures getting closer, Sam decided it was now or never. He held up his lamp to see what he might run into and took off at a breakneck pace. Ahead of him, halfway down, a tunnel wall suddenly collapsed. Dirt, coal and rocks toppled onto the tunnel floor as two of the creatures burst forth. Sam ran up to the closest of the two and punted it in the head, snapping its neck. He leapt over the pile of debris and continued running at a fast pace. The second creature was right behind him, whooping and screaming at. Sam looked ahead. The ray of light still shone from the end of the tunnel. He hoped it emanated from a break in the exterior wall, or else he was a dead man. He bore down and dug deep for any more speed his short legs could manage. The second Pukwudgie was so close behind he could feel its hot, fetid breath on his back. He reached out to the wall ahead of him, grasping at the light beam, and the hope it offered.

Two Trees and Mac squatted in front of the dynamite detonator with the plunger fully extended.

"You or me?" Asked Mac.

"Me."

"I can do it, if it's about Sam."

"Shut up."

Mac backed off. Two Trees grasped the plunger but paused. Was his friend gone? Had he been killed and eaten by the Pukwudgies? Would he resurrect? He wished he had been able to do more for Sam.

"I'm sorry, brother." He shoved the plunger down.

The next thing Sam knew, he was being catapulted through the air as three nearly simultaneous explosions thundered behind him. The dirt wall rushed up at him and he into it. Suddenly, he was in the open air and sunshine. His arms cart wheeled as the explosion blew him out of the mine like a newborn babe being pushed through the thighs of one of Big Laverne's girls. He tumbled through the air amidst rocks, dirt and dust, landing ten feet outside the mine. He slid across the dry earth and came to rest on his back.

"Sam!" Yelled Two Trees.

"Sonofabitch!" Said Mac.

Sam's Pukwudgie pursuer landed a few yards away from him, screaming in pain as its skin began to bubble and smoke. Muscles melted away, sloughing off bones like greasy mucous. It arched its back in agony as smoke rose out of its mouth and nose. It's eyes rolled up white as they momentarily boiled in the sun before exploding. At that, the creature curled into a ball and whimpered quietly as it died.

Two Trees and Mac ran over to Sam and helped him stand up. He was shaky but managed to keep his footing. He looked over at the dead creature as it melted into the hard-packed earth. Two Trees picked him up and gave him a massive bear hug.

"I thought you were dead."

"Me too, but at least the mine exploded."

Mac said, "When we blow things up, we do it right."

Sam looked at the two men. "That was you two?"

"Yup."

"With me still in there?"

"We thought you were dead," said Two Trees.

Sam looked at the two men and then nodded his head in understanding.

He smirked. "Remind me not to get blown up again."

All three of them laughed as they walked back to their horses. Sam stopped for a final look back at the mine. Smoke poured out of its entrance as well as other holes along the ridge.

"Do you think they're all dead?"

"I hope so," said Two Trees. "It is too bad about the miners."

"Hey!" Yelled Mac. "We are not staying! We are leaving right feckin' now!"

Sam and Trees looked at each other and nodded. They laughed all the way to their horses and the cook wagon.

Sam looked at the wagon and felt a pang in his stomach.

"Mac, you any good at cooking? I'm powerfully hungry."

He ducked as a frying pan spun past his head.

The trip back to Wichita usually took two days. Anxious to return, they cut the trip to one-and-a-half by riding hard and skipping a mid-day meal. Once back in town, Mac headed to the livery stables to break down his supplies. Then he fed and brushed out his horses. Later, he'd check back in with the mining company for a new assignment.

Sam and Two Trees went directly to the Wichita Mining Company offices on Wichita Street. They tethered their horses and walked up to the second-floor manager's office.

Sloane Roberts had been good to Sam in the past and never had any problems with hiring on Two Trees as additional muscle. He sat down with the two men and asked how the job went.

"It went to shit," said Sam.

"What do you mean?" Said Roberts.

Sam recalled the trip out and what they discovered upon arriving at the mining camp. He made sure to mention Rhys Macgillicuddy's professionalism, and how they escorted him to and from the mining camp

"What about the miners?" Asked Roberts.

"All dead, sir."

"Dead?"

"Yes, sir."

"What the hell happened?" Asked Roberts, incredulously.

"We do not know sir," said Two Trees.

Roberts stood up with his hands on his desk and yelled, "What do you mean you don't know?"

Sam got to his feet and looked at Roberts. He sat back down, attempting to calm himself.

"I'm sorry, Two Trees. What do you mean they're all dead?"

The giant native straightened up in his chair. "We arrived at the camp to find buildings on fire. The men and livestock were missing and the camp in disarray."

"No signs of the men?"

"There were bodies, sir."

"Where were they?"

"Uh," Two Trees thought back to where they had found the men. "The chow tent, bunkhouses, on the grounds, and in the mine."

"What do you mean, grounds?"

"They were scattered near the camp and down at the mine."

"And they were all dead?"

"Torn apart."

Robert's face started to turn red. "That's a bit different than just dead."

No one said anything for a few seconds.

"Any idea what killed them?"

Sam jumped in. "No, sir."

The mining manager looked from Sam to Two Trees. They remained silent.

"What about the cook?"

"He's fine. We dropped him at the livery stables. He said he'd be right over."

At that moment, as though prearranged, Rhys Macgillicuddy knocked on the open office door and stepped in.

Sam gestured at him. "See? Fine as an Irish fiddle."

Rhys looked at the two men and then back to the manager.

"Good morning, Mister Roberts. Macgillicuddy reportin' in."

"Come in, Rhys."

The cook came in and closed the door.

"Rhys, these gentlemen tell me you found the miners and they were torn apart. Is that true?"

Rhys cleared his throat. "Yes sir."

"Do you know what tore those men apart?"

Rhys looked at Sam and Two Trees, then back to Roberts. "No, sir."

"Are you telling me, that you, a seasoned company cook who has travelled all over the territories, have no idea what killed these men?"

"I wasn't there when they were killed, so no, I have no idea what killed them."

"Hrumpf," mumbled Roberts. "Would any of you like to try and take a guess at what killed them?"

All Roberts heard was the sound of barn crickets. There was no response from any of them. Roberts' face began to look like a ripe tomato. He stood up from his desk, looked down at his blotter and breathed deeply.

Roberts wasn't getting any answers. He decided to just get rid of Sam and Two Trees. "You two get outta my face."

"We'd like to get paid," said Sam.

"Paid! I just lost an entire camp, and you want to get paid?"

"Yes sir. We were hired to escort the cook out to the camp and that is what we did. We also brought him back unharmed. We won't ask ya for additional pay."

"You're not going to ask for extra pay? You're doing me such a huge favor. I should boot you both out of here!"

Two Trees stood and looked down on the manager. "We did what was asked of us. We expect to be paid."

Roberts could barely control himself. His face was now beet red, he pulled at his hair with trembling hands.

He said to Rhys. "And you, what the fuck do you want?"

Rhys looked like he'd been slapped in the face, but he kept his cool. "I'm just here to check in and see where you want me to go next."

"You don't want to get paid?"

"I haven't cooked anything, yet."

Roberts make weird whining noises. He turned and opened a wood file cabinet and removed small bags of coins. He flung them at Sam and Two Trees, then waved them off. "Here's your pay, get outta my face."

Sam said, "What did you expect us to do? The men were dead, we weren't hired for burial duty. We could have left Mac out there by himself."

"I wasn't thrilled about dat idea," said Rhys.

Roberts had enough with the men in his office. "All three of you, get out of my office!"

"But what about my new posting?" Asked Rhys.

"See me next week," said Roberts with an ugly look on his face.

The men left the office and into the street.

"That fecker's never gonna give me work."

"Sorry, Mac."

"Ah, no worries. I'm a good cook. There's plenty of camps around lucky to 'ave me."

"We should be going," said Two Trees.

"You stay outta trouble, Rhys Macgillicuddy," said Sam.

"You too, ya little shit. Stay safe Mister Trees."

Two Trees nodded at the Irishman. He and Sam made their way to Main Street. Sam turned one way, and Two Trees, the other.

"*Nomattimen*, where are you going?"

"Home, to Aponi."

"We've got business at the Pretty Kitty." Said Sam.

"Now?"

"Why not?"

"I don't have all the money with me."

Sam flipped Two Trees his bag of coins. "Then let's get the rest and make you a free man."

"Now?"

"Yes, now. What's the problem?"

"It is a big move."

"One that's a long time coming."

The friends walked to Two Trees' shack. Twenty minutes later they walked through the front door of the Pretty Kitty. Big Laverne was standing at the bar.

Sam patted his friend's shoulder, "You've got this."

Two Trees walked up to Laverne. From where Sam stood, he couldn't hear the conversation, but he saw Two Trees put his money on the bar. It looked like Laverne wasn't too happy about losing her best money-maker. She stopped her wild gesturing, scooped up the money and they walked to her office. Two Trees caught Sam's eye. He pulled his pistol and discreetly held it to his side. At the first sign of trouble, he was going in gun blazing.

Minutes later, Two Trees came from the back with a piece of paper in his hand. Sam took it and read the contract. At the bottom were two signatures and in red ink, the words "Paid in full."

"Congratulations, brother."

"Thank you. Let us go home."

The two men walked out of the saloon and into Two Trees' new life.

Big Laverne stepped out the front doors of the bar and stared at the men walking away. She began to leave the front porch, but the sun was high and her sensitive complexion would burst into flames. She stepped back into the shadows, but her ravishing good looks would always keep her in the forefront. A bartender came to her side, she whispered orders to him, and then he left her alone to think how to balance her books now that the saloon's biggest asset was gone.

My initial idea for this story was of Sam being chased through a cavern and then exploding through the cavern wall to the outside. That was it, but I also wanted to write my own Morlock story. I found the Pukwudgies in my monster research and they were exactly what I needed in the story. The coal mine and the camp came later. Of course Sam had to draw Two Trees into the frey.

With the idea that he could be a free man, Two Trees jumped at the chance, even though his past excursions with Sam had been disasters.

Macgillicuddy was my maternal grandmother's maiden name. It was fun introducing a new character and to learn his voice.

The Roberts character was inspired by actor, Jon Polito, from Miller's Crossing, Barton Fink, Mimic 2 and The Freshman. His hot-headed personality and physical aspects were exactly what I envisioned.

I felt very good about the humor between Sam, Two Trees and Rhys. I felt I did my job in keeping parts of the story light, but then driving it home, especially with the mining managers journal.

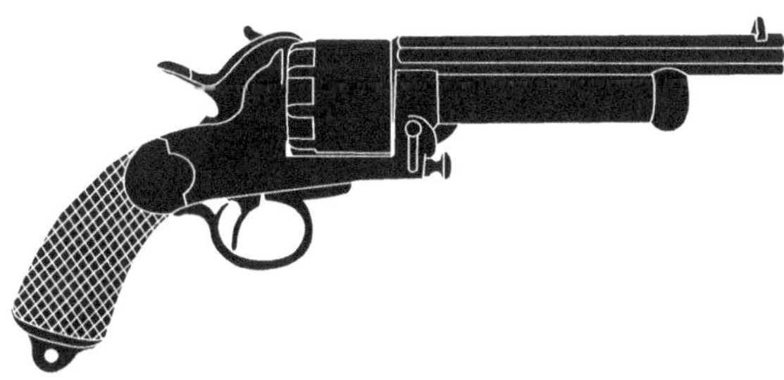

The Last Days of the Pretty Kitty

"Samuel Hawkins?"

Sam froze when he heard his name. He put his beer on the bar and lowered the brim of his hat to hide the cross-shaped scar on his forehead. He turned around slowly. Sheriff Cat Williams stood behind him. Other consumers of beer and hard spirits slowly stepped away from the two men. When Williams came-a-calling, it usually meant you were in trouble.

Sam wanted to distance himself from the Pretty Kitty, so he had started visiting the Rambling Rose at the other end of Wichita's main street.

"Howdy, Sheriff Williams. What can I do for you?" he said, tipping his hat and keeping his hands in plain sight.

"Son, you need to come with me."

No one had called Sam "son" in a long time. Sheriff Williams had a fatherly presence, even though he was a confirmed bachelor. He was of average height, but his stomach showed that he never ate at home and sometimes over-indulged. If you thumped his stomach it sounded like a ripe watermelon. He had a lined face, clear blue eyes and a black handlebar mustache that took some time to oil and wax. He wore a Colt Navy revolver on his hip, but Sam noticed his hand was nowhere near it.

"I'm just wetting my whistle, Sheriff."

"And I'll get you back here as soon as possible, but I need you 'ta take a look at somethin' for me."

Sam looked around. Some faces were watching the discussion, and others had turned away in fear that they might witness something bloody and dangerous.

Sam nodded his head. "Lead the way, Sheriff."

Sam fell in line with Williams. The two men turned down Main Street and walked two blocks up and crossed over one. They stopped in front of a dark alley being guarded by two of the sheriff's deputies, Jeffries and Hastings. Sam knew both of them and held no ill will towards them. They both eyeballed him but made no attempt to take him into custody.

"Sheriff, I don't know what this is all about, but I've been behaving myself."

"Don't worry, Sam, I just need you to look at something for me."

Williams led the way into the alley. Halfway in, a body lay under a grey tarp. Sam quickly thought back over the past few days and came up with no recollection of any fights or shootings. He thought he was okay.

The sheriff nodded to his deputies, and together the two men flipped back the tarp.

Williams asked, "Is this your friend?"

Sam stepped closer and saw that the dead man was huge and had long black hair, although some of it had been ripped out at the roots. He had mahogany colored skin, but his face was a mix of purple bruises, deep brown welts and blood. Lots of blood.

There was only one man he knew of this size and coloring.

"Two Trees?" Sam said softly, eyes instantly tearing. *Two Trees... dead?*

Sam began to kneel beside his friend when Deputy Hastings reached out to stop him.

Williams made a grunting noise and the hand disappeared. Sam knelt beside his friend and looked at the devastation of his face. He raised a corner of the tarp, surprised and saw that Two Trees was naked. His body, like his face, had been beaten over and over until it was covered in bruises. His right arm was bent at a odd angle, broken in at least one place.

Sam looked up at the sheriff. "Have you told Aponi?"

"Who's she?" asked Hastings.

"Aponi Maniwaki, she's his woman. They live in a shack behind Dobbs' Mercantile."

"I know Aponi," said Williams. "She's a bit crazy."

Sam looked at him. "The only thing she's crazy about is this man. What happened to him?"

"No idea," answered the sheriff. Jeffries was in the office when a kid came in and said there was a dead injun in an alley. He came and got me, and I saw who it was. I needed it 'ta be official and have someone else identify him. I knew you two ran together, doing odd jobs and the like."

"And that's why I'm here."

"Yeah."

"Better me than Aponi."

"We didn't need a spectacle in the middle of the street."

Sam looked down at his friend and said a quiet prayer to himself.

"*Kuwumáras*, I hope to see you on the other side, Two Trees."

He placed his hand on his friend's chest when Two Trees

suddenly spit up a gout of blood and then coughed.

"He's choking on his blood. Help me roll him!"

The two deputies stood like rooted trees as Williams and Sam pushed Two Trees onto his side. Blood seeped out of his nostrils and poured from his mouth. Williams patted him on the back clearing his airway. Two Trees took a deep breath, his lungs made a thick gurgling sound, but at least he was breathing.

Sheriff Williams looked to his deputies. "Get me a wagon and horses. We gotta get this man to Doc Walters."

Both men stood there with blank expressions on their faces. "He's gonna die, Sheriff, why bother?" asked Hastings.

"He's just a redskin," said Jeffries.

Sam looked at both deputies. "Move your asses, or I'll shoot both of you where you stand."

Maybe it was the tone, or maybe the electricity running through Sam's bright blue eyes, but it was enough to set the men to action.

"You weren't going to really shoot him, were you son?" asked the sheriff.

"If it meant the life or death of my friend, then I sure as shit would have."

This got Sheriff Williams thinking that he might have been wrong about Sam Hawkins' character.

Jeffries and Hastings soon returned with a horse and buckboard. Sam, Williams and Hastings lifted the huge man and placed him in the back of the wagon. They were as careful as possible. Sam pushed Jeffries aside and took the reins from him. He began to object, but the look Sam gave him made Jeffries think better of it.

Williams and Hastings climbed into the back of the wagon and held Two Trees down so he wouldn't roll around and injure himself further. Sam yanked back on the reins, the horses jumped and the wagon set off down the street. The gathered crowd made way for the wagon.

Doctor Walter Walters' house was off Main Street. He had a large lot and small barn to the rear. Besides being a medical doctor, he had a touch when it came to farm animals. He split his time between two-legged and four-legged patients.

The doctor was standing in his doorway, having been alerted by a rubbernecker. The wagon pulled up to his white picket fence.

"Bring him in here!" he called out.

Two Trees was carried inside to the doctor's examination room, and placed on the exam table. Doc Walters was surprised by the man's size and saw his lower legs hung over the edge of the table. He yelled out to his wife, who was also his nurse: "Mary, bring in the small rolling table from the office."

She appeared seconds later rolling in a wooden table with fancy crocheted doily on it.

"Oh my gosh," Mary Walters said when she saw the mass of man lying on the examination table. Doctor and nurse gently place Two Trees' legs upon the rolling table.

The doctor put on an apron and cloth mask, and took his stethoscope from out of a drawer. He began listening to Two Trees' chest and stomach. He nodded and shook his head as he went along. Williams started asking him questions and the doctor gave him a sharp look that quieted the lawman.

Walters began carefully pressing various points upon the big man's face and skull. He then worked his way down to the man's massive arms and tree-trunk legs. He was respectful of Two Trees' right arm, and gingerly felt along the forearm to see where the break was.

Sam had been to see Doc Walters a few months back. The

doctor helped him as much as he could, but realized that Sam needed spiritual rather than medical help. Sam was very appreciative of the aid he received, and the two men were now on a first name basis.

"Sam, I want you to grip Two Trees' hand. Sheriff, I want you and one of your deputies to hold his shoulder." The three men took their places and Walters urged them to hold on tight. When everyone was ready, the doctor pushed down on the broken forearm until he felt the bones realign. Even though he was semi-conscious, Two Trees still managed to almost shake the lawmen off his shoulder and Sam had to hold on with both hands to steady the arm.

"Thank you, gentlemen. Mary and I will set his arm. We'll treat his open wounds and bleed his bruises. You can wait in our sitting room or make yourselves some coffee in our kitchen."

"Thanks, Doc," said Williams as he and his deputies left the room.

"Sam, you can go with them."

"Thanks, but no. I'll stay here with Two Trees. I got a feeli –"

Before he could finish, Aponi burst into the room and tried to get to her love. Sam held her back and tried to talk her down. He said Two Trees needed medical help and that he would be all right.

She looked at him with anger in her face.

"*Tic-kee, tic-kee!* You say you are his *theemetha*, his brother. Look what your word has done to him."

Sam looked dumbstruck at her, "I wasn't with him."

"Not this time, but because of you, he pay off debt. Then they hurt him."

"Godammit," Sam said quietly.

"Who hurt him, Aponi?" asked Sheriff Williams walking back into the room.

Aponi looked at the lawman and tried to hide her distrust. "Nobody. Nobody hurt Two Trees. He must have fell."

Williams could smell pig shit when he smelled it, so he turned to Sam and asked him, "Hawkins, who hurt Two Trees? Who did he pay a debt off to?"

Sam looked at Williams, and then he looked at Aponi. She had that look on her face that said, *'If you say it your balls are mine',* and *'Please don't stir up any trouble.'*

Sam said, "I don't know who would want to hurt Two Trees, sir."

He looked at them and his expression showed disappointment. "Oh, that's how it's going to be. Okay you two, this isn't over," he said, pointing his finger at them. "Something is rotten and I will find out what it is."

Williams left with his deputies, leaving the doctor, Aponi and Sam with Two Trees.

"Mary, can you come here?" asked Walters.

"Yes, doctor?"

"Please take these two into the kitchen and get them some coffee. Then come back and help me treat this man."

"Yes, doctor. Come with me." she said to Aponi and Sam. They followed her to the kitchen.

While Mary brewed the coffee, Doctor Walters began cleaning Two Trees' wounds. He checked his pulse and breathing. Walters had never seen anyone beaten so badly and not be dead. He chalked it up to the man's muscular build and tolerance for pain. A lesser man would have succumbed to these kinds of wounds. He'd be preparing a funeral, not an examination.

When Mary came back from the kitchen, they began to undress the large man. His tassel buckskin pants had to be cut off. His swollen left knee looked like a spoiled sausage. Two

Trees had a native wrap around his privates. When the doctor removed it, he was shocked by what he found. The man's testicles were swollen and looked like two large plums. Someone had focused their beating on his testicles, luckily his penis was undamaged. The doctor was shocked by the size of it. When Mary came over with a damp cloth and saw Two Trees third leg, she blushed and turned away. She was a trained nurse, but some things should not be seen by proper ladies.

Doc moved back to Two Trees' swollen knee and pointed out marks on it.

"What are those, Walter?" asked Mary.

"Those are boot prints. Someone stomped on his knee over and over. They were looking to maim him, they wanted to make sure he never walked again."

"My God, who would do that?"

"Someone who enjoyed delivering pain."

They finished removing Two Trees' clothes. Mary began bleeding Two Trees' larger hematomas. Doctor Walters examined the rest of his body for any other injuries and began stitching up the deeper lacerations.

Sam and Aponi sat in silence at the kitchen table, drinking coffee and looking everywhere but at each other. Sam explained to Aponi about the agreement Two Trees and he made to clear his debt. Aponi wouldn't hear of it. They remained in silence. Sam slumped on the table, quietly drinking coffee while Aponi sat, with her coffee untouched. Her eyes were closed and her back was straight as a rod.

Mary came into the kitchen, "The doctor will see you now."

Sam stood and looked at Aponi. Her eyes opened and he saw how red and moist they were. She was not one to show her emotions, but this made him rethink his opinion of her. They walked back to the examination room and Doctor Walters had them sit down on two wooden chairs.

"First, I'll tell you that Two Trees will live." A quick flush of relief came across their faces, "But it's going to be a long recuperation. Most of his injuries will heal and not affect his quality of life. However, his right arm was severely broken. We have the bones back in place and put a plaster of Paris cast on it. I'll want to have you bring him back in two weeks for a follow-up examination.

"How long will he need cast?" asked Aponi.

The doctor smiled at her, "It takes six to eight weeks for the bones to completely mend. Then a few weeks for the muscles to regain their full strength."

"Ten weeks," Sam said.

"Yes, I feel by then he'll be completely healed. He might still be weak, but he's strong and fit. After the cast comes off, he could return to work."

"He is not working now," said Aponi with a sharp glance at Sam.

"I thought he worked at the Pretty Kitty?"

Sam looked at the doctor, "Two Trees paid off his debt and quit them."

"What kind of work was he doing?"

Aponi said nothing, so it was left to Sam.

"He worked as... um... "

Aponi had no patience for niceties. "He had sex with women who could pay for it."

"Oh my." said Mary Walters, thinking back to the size of Two Trees' penis.

"If it's what he wanted –"

"It's not what he wanted," said Sam. "He was a slave in Florida and when President Lincoln freed them in '63, he tried to leave. His owners wouldn't let him go. Somehow the Pretty

Kitty heard about his unique… ahem, male feature. They bought out his debt. He became an indentured servant."

"When will he come home?" Aponi asked.

"I think," said Walters, "a couple of days. He's still out cold, he needs to rest. I want to make sure his head injuries have no complications. Mary is going to make some of her famous broth. It will give him the strength he needs to heal."

Aponi stood and went to the doctor. "*Neia* doctor, for saving my husband." She took his hands and kissed them. This display of thanks surprised the doctor.

"No need for thanks, Aponi, this is my job. I'll make sure he recovers."

"Can I stay with him?" asked Aponi.

The doctor shook his head. "He's still unconscious. I want to make sure he's fully awake before I send him home. He'll need his rest, and you will too. Come back tomorrow after breakfast and I'll update you."

"Thanks, Doc," said Sam.

"Are you going to come by?"

Sam looked at Aponi and weighed his options. "This is a family thing; I think I'll wait until he gets home."

Two Trees stayed at Doctor Walters' office for three days. He regained consciousness after day one, and the doctor was watching him for any signs of a concussion. He was able to sit up and keep down Mary's healing broth. He slept through most of the second day. When he awoke later that evening, Aponi was there by his side. She took his large hand in both of hers and kissed it profusely.

"Thank the Great Tribes. I prayed to them for days, *Munumayenok*, for your recovery."

"No need… to worry, *Nunaumonittumwos*, my wife. I already... feel better."

Doctor Walters came over to his patient. "Hello, Two Trees, how are you feeling?"

"Much... better, doctor."

"That's good to hear. I am prescribing bed rest for a week. I want you to stay off your knee. I've wrapped it and you can put cold, soaked wraps on it to help with the swelling."

"I have some balms I can rub on his knee to help," said Aponi.

"I appreciate the help, Aponi." Walters said. He directed his attention to Two Trees. "I want you to take it easy. You've got a broken arm and it will take time to heal."

"Yes, doctor."

"That's what I like to hear. Aponi, I want him to stay until tomorrow and then you can take him home."

"But Doctor, he is awake, he is ready... "

" One more night, Aponi, then the patient is all yours."

"I do not think I like how that sounds." said Two Trees.

Later that night, Doctor Walters took his wife out to dinner after feeding Two Trees. While he was resting, Two Trees heard a tapping at the door. Sam stepped into the house, nodding at his friend.

"Where's Aponi?" Sam quietly asked, looking around the room.

"She is home, preparing for my homecoming."

"Can I come in?"

"Of course, you are my *theemetha*. You are always welcome."

"If Aponi was here, I wouldn't be. She's angry at me."

Sam came into the room and pulled up a chair next to the bed.

"Why? You saved my life. My spirit felt you near by. That helped me return from the Camp of the Dead."

Sam smirked and rubbed his chin. "Because I helped you pay off your debt, she blames me for the beating."

"Sam, that is silly."

"To you and me it's silly. To Aponi I am *moinguena*, shit-face."

"It is still silly."

"You explain it to her, then come see me."

"Hmm, maybe."

Sam drew his chair closer.

"Brother, what happened. Who beat you?"

Two Trees was hesitant to say, but if there was anyone he could trust, it was Sam.

"There were four of them. They followed me after the saloon closed."

"Were they from the Pretty Kitty?" Sam asked.

Two Trees was silent.

"Was it Cody and Deacon from the second floor?"

Two Trees remained silent, but his body language said it all.

"Those slabs of meat will get theirs. Who else?"

Two Trees did not look up, but muttered under his breath. "Morris and Renee."

"I know Morris from the bar, but I don't know Renee."

"He is a worm," Two Trees said. "He works in the back with the special people and is very cruel. I saw him beating Lulu and taunting the dead women."

"Lulu," Sam said quietly.

The men sat in silence for minutes.

Then Sam made a decision. "When they find out you're alive, you think they'll come for you?"

"I hope not, but I would not put it past them."

"I've met men like them. They'll be back."

"Then I will have to be ready for them."

Sam stood and put his hand on his friends shoulder.

"Don't worry, I'll take care of them."

"Sam, I do not want you to get in trouble."

Sam smiled, "Trouble is my middle name."

Two Trees went home later the next day. Aponi had rearranged their entire home so he would be more comfortable. The kitchen table and furniture had been moved to the walls and their bed had been turned so he could navigate the room easier.

Two Trees didn't tell her about the conversation he had with Sam. He did not want her to worry. Sam assured Two Trees that they would be safe.

Three days later, Aponi was running errands for the house. She had stopped by the general market to buy essentials, then to the butcher down on Second Street. She wanted a nice piece of beef to help build Two Trees' strength up.

On her way home, she took a shortcut behind the butchers and ran into Cody, one of the bouncers from the Pretty Kitty.

"Hello, squaw. What are you doing here?"

Aponi stopped in her tracks and squinted her eyes at him.

"Leave me alone. Get out of my way."

"Still got a mouth on you. It's a shame about your injun, him not here to protect you."

"Leave me alone," said Aponi, her voice quivering.

Cody walked toward her, rolling up his sleeves, exposing tightly muscled forearms.

Aponi backed down the alley when she heard footsteps behind her. She turned and Deacon, the other bouncer, was standing behind her. He was grinding his fist in the palm of his other hand.

"It's too bad no one's here ta help ya," he said as he walked towards her. Aponi found herself trapped between the two men with no means of escape. Deacon walked by stacked crates as a shadow detached itself from the wall.

"Cody, what should we show her first, what a broken jaw feels like, or broken ribs?" asked Deacon.

"What about a fractured skull?" came a question from the shadows.

Deacon turned and Sam stepped forward, swinging a two-by-four at his head. He smashed the back of Deacon's skull and sprayed blood against the wall. The big bouncer croaked out a yell and staggered forward. He tried to right himself when Sam charged and swung the board between his legs. Deacon's testicles were crushed and he was lifted off the ground.

Deacon collapsed on the ground with a *"whoof,"* and stopped moving.

Aponi was horrified by the violence as Sam walked past her, board in his hand.

"What the hell did you do ta Deacon?" yelled Cody.

"What you should be asking is, *what am I going to do to you?*" Sam said pointing the bloody piece of lumber.

Cody looked at his friend on the ground, then he saw the glare in Sam's eyes. He turned and ran. Sam reached into his vest's collar and pulled out his brand-new throwing knife. He flipped his arm out and a fang of steel flew, sinking into Cody's shoulder .

The pain drove the big man forward into the dirt. As he tried to get up, Sam swept his leg with the board, dumping him onto his back. The knife ramming further into his shoulder. Cody screamed into the air. Sam drove the end of the board into Cody's stomach, and he folded into a ball of pain.

Cody's face was contorted, as tears welled out of his eyes and beads of sweat popped up on his face.

"What... do you want... ?"

"I think the question is – what do you want?

"What I want... is to live."

"Well, that will cost extra, and you know, '*Anything you want inside is extra.*'"

Upon hearing his own words, Cody knew his goose was cooked. Sam swung the board so hard, two things broke: Cody's skull and then the board.

The broken piece of two-by-four shot into the air and Cody collapsed onto the ground. The front of his skull was caved in, his eyes bulged and blood leaked out of his nose and ears.

Sam stared down at the dead man, taking in all the violence he had caused.

From behind him, he heard, "Sam?"

The resurrected man turned and saw Aponi cringing against the brick wall of the butcher's shop. She was staring at him, and the blood splattered on his shirt. Then she looked at the two men on the ground; one dead and the other slowly dying.

Sam walk over to the dead man, *"What was his name, Cody?"* and pulled his knife from the man's back. He walked passed Aponi, and she couldn't see his beautiful blue eyes. They were buried in shadows.

Sam walked over to Deacon, still writhing in pain from his groin.

"Who ordered you to hurt, Two Trees?"

It took Deacon a minute to comprehend the question.

"Laverne."

Sam nodded and asked, "Who ordered you to hurt Lulu?"

Deacon looked up as blood ran from his head wound.

He sighed. "Laverne."

"Thank you," said Sam.

He shoved his throwing knife into the man's ear. Deacons' screams rang out along the alley. The knife pierced his brain, insuring there wouldn't be another undead walking around town.

Sam dropped the board, walked by Aponi and down the alley. "Don't rush home. I'll have some tidying up to do."

Two Trees was just waking from his midday nap, when he heard a noise in the front room of the shack. He threw off the light quilt covering his legs and listened.

There it was again.

"Aponi?"

He didn't get an answer. He swung his legs off the bed and grabbed the crutch Aponi made for him. He maneuvered his way to the doorway and looked into the kitchen. No one was there, so he peeked into the living area. The door was wide open and Renee from the Pretty Kitty was there, but he wasn't alone. He had one of the undead women from the saloon secured by a catch pole by its neck. As soon as she saw Two Trees, she lunged but Renee had a strong grip on the wood pole.

Two Trees backed into the doorway. It seemed the management of the saloon still wanted their revenge on him. Renee was going to be his punisher.

"Hey big boy, I heard you weren't feeling well. I brought ya a present. Isn't she sweet?"

"Get out of my house." The big man said.

"This ain't no house, this is a shithole."

Two Trees' mind began to race, he needed to know one thing.

"Where is Aponi?"

"Your squaw? Right now I imagine Cody and Deacon have had their way with her. They're cutting her into little pieces."

"Goddamn you!" Two Trees charged the man, but the

undead woman blocked his path. He swung the homemade crutch at her, connecting with the side of her face. All it did was make the thing angry. Two Trees lost his balance and fell in the kitchen. He looked over and the woman was creeping towards him. Two Trees scrambled away from her, putting the kitchen table between them.

"You can keep trying to hide, but sooner or later my friend is going to start chewin' on that bum knee of yours. Then she'll work her way to your black sausage. She'll keep going until there's nothin' left of ya."

"Oh, Aponi... my love," said Two Trees, with ache in his heart and tears in his eyes.

"Don't get all weepy, injun. Cody and Deacon will take good care of your squaw." said Renee.

"But who's going to take care of Cody and Deacon?"

Renee turned and caught a pistol barrel in the face. That dropped him to the ground.

"Hey, dead bitch!" yelled Sam. The undead woman turned and saw Renee on the floor.

He had dropped the catch pole and that allowed her to move on him.

"No... no... keep away... " weeped Renee.

He looked at Sam standing in the doorway. He had blood splattered all over him.

"Wha... didja... do? Asked Renee.

"I taught them they shouldn't hurt women."

Sam heard the quiet sigh of relief escape Two Trees' lips.

Renee screamed as the undead woman began chewing his face. He stopped when she tore out his throat. She deserved revenge for the nightmare that Renee and the others had put her through.

Sam aimed his pistol at her head, cocked it, "I suppose I should put her outta –

The rifle shot barked from behind him and he felt the slug slice through his right shoulder.

"Goddamnit!" he yelled, falling forward. He leapt clear of the feast before him and veered away from the open door.

"Renee, you okay?"

Two Trees caught Sam's eye, he mouthed, 'Morris.'

Sam put his hand on his shoulder and pulled away blood, it wasn't bad.

Sam turned his head. "Morris, I'm fine! You should see what my bitch is doing in here."

"Did I get the cowpoke?"

"Ya sure did. Come see."

Sam heard footsteps scuff through the dirt and pound up the wood stairs that led to the front door. Morris burst into the living room and saw the horror of Renee being eaten by one of the undead. She had stripped off his face, ripped out his throat down to the spine and was starting on his shoulder.

"My God… Renee… "

"Looks like she was hungry," said Sam from behind Morris. "I betcha she still is." Sam clubbed Morris on the back of the neck with his pistol and Morris dropped, landing on Renee.

The undead woman looked at what landed in front of her, then glanced at Sam with a grunt.

"Go ahead, it's all yours."

As the woman tore into Morris' ear, Sam kicked the front door closed, walked around the mess and sat next to Two Trees.

"How are you doin', *qunnuhquitugk*?"

Two Trees looked at Sam and chuckled. "My 'tall tree' is just fine. Is Aponi, okay?"

"She's fine, a bit scared.She should be here soon. I wanted to be here first to take care of business."

"But how?"

"I've been following her every time she went out, making sure she was safe. When I saw Cody and Deacon make their move, I figured the other two would be here, lookin' for you."

"Thank you, my brother." said Two Trees.

Sam glanced at the horrific scene in the living room. "Let me clean this mess up before your wife comes home."

Sam dispatched the undead woman with a shot from his pistol.

He dragged the three bodies out the backdoor of the shack. Then stole some tarps from the hardware store down the street. Sam retrieved his packhorse Larry from the livery stables and dragged the bodies a mile out of town to a small ravine he knew. All three bodies went in and Sam stomped along the sandy edge dislodging dirt and stones. A small landslide buried them.

He stood next to Larry and stroked his head and muzzle.

"You're a good boy, aren't ya'?"

Larry nuzzled him and brayed his lips, smiling.

Sam laughed and held the dear horse's head in his arms. He kissed his forehead, then slipped a carrot out of his vest pocket. He held it in front of the horse and it disappeared faster than it appeared.

"I'm going to miss you so much."

Sam walked through the backdoor of the shack and saw Two Trees was at the kitchen table.

"You okay?"

"I am fine. Just waiting for a storm to walk in the door."

Two Trees pointed at the enormous blood stain on the floor.

"I've got this." Sam said.

He took out a wood bucket and filled it with fresh water from the pump. He retrieved a bag of baking soda and a gallon of vinegar he had stashed behind the shack. In fifteen minutes, the spot was almost gone. Sam cleaned the bucket and the scrubbing brush he used.

"You will make a woman very happy, someday."

Sam smirked at his friend. He realized he needed to leave.

"How can I thank you?" asked Two Trees.

Sam leaned against the sink. "Any other time, I would say no thanks needed... "

"But... "

"But now I need your help in taking down the Pretty Kitty. Once I've done that, you need to leave town."

"I don't know how I can help," he said gesturing to his broken arm and ruined knee.

"It will take three of us for my plan to come together."

Two Trees began to respond, when Sam pushed off from the sink. He went to a large rug and moved it over the drying spot. "Think it over. It's not a big deal, but a necessary one."

He left through the backdoor, seconds before Aponi came in the front door.

Two days later, Sam was sitting on the stairs to the shack, when Aponi opened the door. She had a broom to sweep off the landing. He held up his trail cup full of coffee and a brown bag full of corn cakes.

"I brought breakfast."

"Come in, *wematin*."

As he walked by, she kissed her fingertip and placed it on Sam's crucifix scar.

Smiling at her, Sam said, "*Meegwetch*."

"You're welcome."

Sam walked in and saw Two Trees sitting at the kitchen table. He sat down and opened the bag of cakes.

"Good morning, brother."

"*Kwey*, Sam."

"How are you?"

"Much better. The cast comes off tomorrow."

"That's great news."

Aponi sat down next to her husband while Sam nibbled on a corn cake.

"Go ahead and eat."

Not a word was spoken as they ate. Sam had a smile on his face, Two Trees wondered what Sam's plan was. Aponi was torn between liking the strange man and kicking him out of their lives.

Sam drank his cup dry. "I need you to help me take down the Pretty Kitty."

"What is your plan?" asked two Trees.

"And how can we help?" asked Aponi.

That surprised Sam, then he told them his plan. When it came to their parts, he spelled them out and waited for their answer.

"That is it?" asked Two Trees.

"Yeah."

"Wait for your signal, and then we leave town?"

"Neither of you will be at risk, 'cause no one will see you. All their eyes will be on me."

"The center of attention."

"That's why I love you, brother. You know me so well."

They laughed at the joke, while Aponi shook her head.

"This is a stupid plan."

Two Trees looked at her and raised his eyebrows in question.

"Will you be able to drive the buckboard?" she asked, resigning to the facts in front of her.

"No problem."

She looked at Sam, "Two days?"

He nodded.

Aponi had a look of frustration on her face. She couldn't make up her mind.

Sam said, "For Two Trees, and for Lulu".

"Yes," Aponi said immediately. "Yes," said Two Trees.

"Great. See you in two days. 6:00 pm at the livery stable." Sam took his coffee cup and left them to talk between themselves.

The next night, Sam was behind the Pretty Kitty, waiting. He didn't have long to wait, when Rosie walked down the alley to the saloon's backdoor.

"Psst."

Rosie lifted her head and looked around. She saw a shadow beckon to her. Rosie was sweet and loving, but not stupid. She had an 1866 double barrel derringer in her clutch. It was a dangerous little weapon, with a white horn grip and beautiful engraving all over it. She quietly palmed it.

"Who's there?"

"Your lover boy." He stepped out of the shadows and smiled at her.

"Sammy!" she said and skipped over to him. She put away the pistol. "You know I'm not supposed to see my "friends" outside the club. Where ya been?"

"You know me, keeping busy. Trying to earn Gold Eagles."

"Do you have any of those Eagles for me, tonight?" as she ran her painted finger along his arm.

"I can't tonight, darlin'. I got a job to do, and that's why I'm here."

He reached out and held her shoulders, maybe a bit harder than he should have. He needed to show her how serious he was.

"Are ya' workin' tomorrow night?"

"Of course silly, it's Friday. All the miners and cowboys will have been paid. I might be sore the next day, but my purse will be full."

"Don't go to work tomorrow night."

"What do you mean don't go to work. Are you crazy?"

"Just a little bit, but I'm also crazy over you. I don't want you to get hurt."

Who's going ta' hurt me here?" Rosie said and waved at the building.

"Please, honey, don't be here tomorrow."

"Sam Hawkins, what have you been drinking? I gotta work to make a livin'!"

Sam realized he was shaking her.

"Sam, honey, why don't you come inside with me. We'll talk about this?"

"No!" said Sam, releasing her and stepping away.

"I'm here to warn you, don't be here."

He pulled a canvas bag from his back pocket and tossed it to her. She grabbed it, heard it clink, and felt the weight of it.

"What's this?"

"That's what I could scratch together. I hope it's enough to change your mind."

Rosie opened the bag and spilled out a small pile of Golden Eagles into her palm.

"Sam, I don't know what to say."

He looked at her and knew she wouldn't listen.

"Don't say anything, just don't be here." He turned and crept back into the shadows, leaving her standing alone.

The following night, Two Trees and Aponi joined Sam at the Wichita Livery Stables. He'd been there an hour before his friends arrived. *Old Indian Trick.* He'd brushed both Sweetie and Larry, fed them sweet alfalfa and treated them to carrots and apples.

The couple approached and watched as he tended to his horses. They saw the love between them and didn't want to interrupt a tender moment. Out of the corner of his eye, Sam saw them and nodded. They sat and went over the final plan for the evening. Sam was cryptic in the full details of it. He just wanted them to be ready to do their part at his signal. They sat for a while and talked, then sat in silence with their thoughts. Sam excused himself and went into Larry's stall. After several minutes he came out wearing his hat and a long duster coat. He was carrying a wooden box and a coil of wire over his shoulder.

He looked at them, "Let's go."

He turned and went out the back of the stables without looking back at his horses. He walked along the backs of buildings until he turned up a short alley. He took up a position behind a stack of crates. The alley opened to Main Street, directly across from the Pretty Kitty.

Aponi looked at her husband as they trailed behind Sam.

"Is he alright?"

Two Trees looked at his wife, "He is a man on a mission and nothing will stop him."

Sam put the wood box down and unraveled the wire coil. He bent down, fumbled with the top of the box and waited for his friends to catch up.

Two Trees stood next to his friend and without looking at him, spoke.

"There is no other way?"

"No."

"I can not talk you out of this?"

"No."

Aponi was getting scared. She had known Sam for three years and he was always talkative. For him to answer questions with just one word, made her think that an *otshee monetoo*, evil spirit, had replaced him at the Camp of the Dead. That the real Sam was still there.

Sam said, "Let it trail out behind me and watch for my signal." The front of the Pretty Kitty was all hand-lettered glass windows advertising the saloon. At night, with the lights on, you could see everything that was happening in the front room. All the private areas were upstairs behind closed doors and in the special bunkhouse.

Sam turned and looked at his giant friend. "Goodbye, my brother." They shook hands. Sam had to shut down his emotions. He needed to be stone-cold for this to work. If not, he'd wet himself and ride off for Canada.

He turned to Aponi, "Goodbye, *wetompasin*, my sister."

Aponi nodded, then like she had done countless of times, she kissed her fingertip and placed it on Sam's scar. Then she touched Two Trees' forehead, then her own.

"We are *elakómkwik*, family, Sam Hawkins. Safe travels."

He smiled at this woman, who always treated him like an outsider, but welcomed him for his heart and the friendship he shared with her husband. He would miss both of them very much.

He stepped around the crates and crossed the street towards the saloon. The wire coil played out from Two Trees' hands as Sam stepped up the front stairs. Without hesitation, he stepped into Hell.

Inside, he left the doors open and looked around. There were two bartenders behind the bar. Their hair greased, mustaches trimmed, wearing white shirts with vests and string ties. Sam guessed there were seventy-five men and women in the front room, all laughing, and drinking. He saw Big Laverne in the back, bustling a half-naked girl into a room. The piano player on his right was banging on the keys like a demon. His tip bowl was already half full. On any other night, the musician would go home happy, but tonight would be different. Tonight, a dead man walked through the doors, and he had mischief on his mind.

Sam looked for the best spot for his needs and saw an empty table towards the center of the room. There were empty beer mugs and shot glasses, but no one was seated. He walked into the room, glancing behind at the trailing wire. He stepped on a chair and took a perch on the table. A few people looked at him, but most of them were two sheets to the wind. They carried on with their drinking.

It wasn't until he started shouting that people took notice.

Two Trees and Aponi stood across the street and saw him ascend the table and wave his hands around. They couldn't hear what he was saying, but they hoped he was giving them a fair piece of his mind.

"Hello cocksuckers and suckers of cock! My name is Resurrection Sam and I wanted to come in tonight and say hello to you all!"

Sam had taken his hat off and those closest saw the scar on his forehead. They all had heard the rumors, and some of them had witnessed one of his resurrections right here in the saloon. He had their attention, so now it was time for him to make it count.

"I wanted to tell you a quick story about the people who work here! There *were* Cody and Deacon –" at hearing their names, Big Laverne glanced up. She looked around to see two of her new bouncers watching Sam. Their jaws were hanging open, catching flies. One of them caught her look and she sharply waved them at Sam. They moved on him, ready to bust heads.

"Cody and Deacon were stupid muscle and they tried to kill some of my friends on the orders of Big Laverne – then there were Renee and Morris. Now Renee was a nasty sort. He used to beat some of the women and tortured the dead girls out back. Morris liked to water down your drinks and he sometimes added a little of his own water to your pours."

Sam saw the new slabs of meat moving his way, so he decided to pick up the pace.

"I just wanted to let you know who you pay your good money to and how they treat some of the lovelies that take your minds off things." He addressed the crowd and more of them were paying attention to him.

He licked his lips and glanced upwards and saw Rosie standing on the second-floor balcony. She looked down at him. He frowned, shook his head, and glanced down for a second or two.

"I just want to say that this shithole needs to be shut down, and all the rats need to be kicked in the ass and sent out the door!"

More of the crowd had stopped drinking and started casting sharp glances at Big Laverne and the bartenders. Sam unbuttoned his duster, throwing it off his shoulders showing everyone his vest made of sticks of dynamite wrapped around his chest. Those patrons closest to him lurched to their feet and put some distance between them and the crazy man on the table.

Two Trees and Aponi watched all this from the street and when Sam unveiled his big surprise, Two Trees heard a slight gasp come from his wife. He picked up the wooden box and placed it on a crate in front of him. Aponi had no idea what it was until her husband pulled the plunger handle up and waited.

Sam pulled Rosie's two-shot derringer out of his pants pocket. She gasped when she saw it. She never saw him palm it from her the other night. He put the barrel to his temple and threw back his other arm.

"My name is Resurrection Sam Hawkins, and I hope not to see any of you sumbitches on the other side!" He pulled the trigger of the gun sending a .410 birdshot round through his skull. His head jerked to the side, and he collapsed onto the table.

Patrons of the bar began to cautiously inch forward. Some chuckled that the dead man went without them. A couple of them looked down and saw the fuse wire, trailing out the door. They realized their night was over.

Two Trees began to push the plunger handle down but stopped. His friend was dead, he wasn't sure he could go through with it. Aponi put her hand on his, and Two trees smiled at her as together, they shoved the detonator handle down.

The Pretty Kitty exploded.

The glass windows blew out first, pelting the buildings on the other side of the street with shards of glass. Two Trees and Aponi quickly ducked down behind the crates as the glass flew their way. The explosion blew upwards taking the second and third floors. Everyone in the saloon had been obliterated. That's why Sam shot himself first. He could take pain, and had felt it many times over. He knew being blasted apart was something he could not endure.

The fire immediately started, and the ruptured gas lines caught and spread fiery destruction all throughout the building.

The inferno spread to the rear bunkhouse and the special people.

Two Trees and Aponi looked over the crate and saw the burning building while pieces of timber, framing, and glass flew into the sky and began littering the street. There were a few businesses nearby and they all suffered explosion and fire damage, but luckily no human casualties.

The couple turned and walked down the alley, arm in arm, and quietly said goodbye to their friends from across the street. Two Trees knew what went on at the Pretty Kitty and he had no tears for most of them.

The wreckage of the Pretty Kitty smoldered for days after the explosion. The volunteer firefighters worked as hard as they could to put out the fire before it spread to other parts of the town. If it were up to most, they would have idly stood by and watched the building burn, not lifting one bucket of water.

Here and there small flare-ups occurred due to buried embers. Local neighbors were watching and put them out. Daily traffic around the ruins continued, but no one took any interest in clearing away the wreckage. Management of the saloon had disappeared. Those employees that survived, had moved on to other saloons and businesses in Wichita.

The employees that were considered unusual, like the bearded and leather ladies, had moved on to other towns. The few remaining oddities like the undead women and the last mountain woman had escaped. The undead were hunted down and destroyed while the *Saskehavas* had run for the high forests in search of her tribe.

Two Trees Holmes and his wife Aponi Maniwaki travelled up Main Street from their shack. They had bought one Morgan horse to work alongside Larry, to haul a small covered wagon. Sweetie, Sam's favorite riding horse, was tied to the back of the wagon and she happily trotted along. They weren't sure if they would keep her or turn her loose to roam free on the plains. They had loaded all of their belongings in the wagon and were heading out of town, north to the Dakotas or possibly Canada. Both were tired of the heat and sand and wanted to feel lush green grass between their toes. The couple wanted to live out their remaining years together, in peace and quiet. Two Trees' wounds had healed but he would always walk with a limp. His broken arm would always tell him when a storm was coming. Aponi was happy that her husband had survived and was willing to leave an occupation he had toiled at for years. They would stop at Sioux City, Iowa to visit with some of her family, before turning north and starting their new life.

Two Trees pulled the team up in front of the ruins of the brothel. He sadly looked about the burnt timbers and ruined structure. He hated it but loved the family that he made while working inside of it. He got to thinking about his *thee-metha*, his brother, and the sacrifice he made to avenge the beating that Two Trees took. He firmly believed Lulu was on Sam's mind when he put his plan into action to destroy this house of evil. She was there for Sam when he battled the Crackling Dead. The giant native was sure Sam hoped that the mountain woman was happy being a mother to their child. Two Trees had guessed that the father was Sam, but he was unsure if the two races could have been compatible. Only nature, fate, and *Gitche Manitou* would know for sure.

He would miss his little brother, but he hoped Sam found his final resting place. Two Trees had witnessed some of Sam's resurrections and they usually took no more than a few hours. It had been days since the explosion and Sam had not appeared. Two Trees and Aponi both believed that there would not be enough of him left to resurrect. It still didn't help the hurting he felt. For some reason, Larry and Sweetie seemed to drift towards the rubble. There was no way they could know that their former owner had died there, but still, the connection between man and animal can be very strong.

Two Trees pulled the reins and the Morgan's started down the road. Sweetie fell in behind the wagon, slipping a few glances towards the remains of the building.

"Goodbye, my brother," said the giant.

Aponi leaned into her husband, put an arm through his and held him tight. She knew what Sam meant to him, and even though she didn't care for him, she was proud of some of the things he did for others during his life.

The covered wagon wound its way out of town, and the couple waved goodbye to people they knew. As the day went on, groups of travelers came through town while the locals went about their everyday business. Train service continued as normal with newspaper editor Marshall Murdock exclaiming how good service had been in his editorial column in the Wichita Daily Beacon. The newspaper had also done a deep dive on the explosion of the Pretty Kitty. Sheriff Williams was quoted , 'At this time we have no clue what happened or who was involved.'

As the day passed and the sun started to set, town folks and visitors started to retreat to their homes or rooms. Since the destruction of the Pretty Kitty, other saloons and men's lounges had picked up in business almost twenty percent. To draw in those customers, saloons were getting creative with their specials and hospitalities.

As dusk came to Wichita, a lone horseman rode down the main street of town. He neither looked around nor acknowledged anyone. Those shopkeepers sweeping up their stoops turned away from the stranger out of fear and disgust. The smell of the rider and his steed was intolerable. No one wanted any trouble, so they let him pass through.

Lieutenant Ambrose Mace, formerly of the 1st Battalion, Trans-Mississippi Confederate Cavalry, rode his undead horse through the center of town. He cared not who was looking at him. He had one reason for this visit to Wichita and was going to accomplish it, undisturbed.

His mount made some ghastly bowel remarks that reminded him it was almost time for a new steed. This one had served its purpose, but unlike him, it was quickly rotting away.

He pulled up in front of the wreckage of the Pretty Kitty and sat in his saddle. Mace stared at the smoking timbers, the scorched wallpaper, ruined carpeting and furniture. There were shards of glass all over the ground and ruptured gas lines strewn about.

Mace leaned forward and listened for any signs of life. He watched for any movement in the rubble. He'd hoped that his curse would end tonight, but he was sadly mistaken. Nothing moved except for the popping of red, hot embers and the occasional flare-up from trapped pockets of gas. He looked up and saw a colony of bats making it's way down from the low hills. They were looking for insects drawn to the outdoor lights, hoping for a bountiful feast. He listened to the chitterings the animals made and tried to remember what it was like to enjoy these simple things. His current life had no joy, no love, and no passion. He had a drive to travel the territories in search of a resurrected man and to consume flesh. He wasn't sure if killing Hawkins would end his life. It was just something he was compelled to do, and now his one hope was gone. No one could have survived that explosion, and he had no feeling of the man's spark.

He tugged the reins and turned his horse towards the setting sun and rode out of town. He still did not care who saw him, for he hoped he would never come through this town again.

Mace turned his head and looking back. The muscles and tendons of his neck stretched and pulled with a creaking sound. There was no moisture in these flexible cords and eventually they would snap off his yellowing bones, impairing his range of motion.

"Goddamn you… Sam Hawkins," the dead man said quietly.

He kicked with his spurs and the horse started to gallop out of town. He no longer wanted to be among people unless needed. All he wished was for Death to chase him down on it's own pale horse, and end his suffering.

The talk of the town the next day would be of the arrival of the dead man. The one who said nothing, ignored everyone, and yet it seemed like he paid his respects at the wreckage of the saloon. He rode his horse hard out of town and did not look back.

What the town missed was the low rumble coming from under the wreckage. It sounded like pieces of rubble settling. Sand began to flow and small pebbles rolled away from one particular spot. Scorched pieces of timber, carpeting and bedding, began to bulge upward.

Something broke the surface of the rubble. It was a battered human hand. Scorched, lacerated with one finger bent backwards at it's smallest joint. The hand rested, as if the exertion to come this far, had depleted it's unnatural energy. It began to tremble and spasm as some of the deeper cuts healed. Healthy skin began to replace the burned tissue and the broken finger repaired itself with a snap. In one final push the hand reached up and sought to grasp the full moon. From deep underground, a quiet noise, almost a whisper, was uttered –

"That was a stupid plan."

This one started with just the title, and grew from there. Sam was righting a wrong and it was only going to be about Lulu, but then I felt it needed to be deeper. That's how Two Trees got involved and I had to beat the shit out of one of my favorite characters.

This story shows the dark side of Sam Hawkins, but it also shows he has a heart when he tries to warn Rosie.

The Pretty Kitty started out as a silly name, but as the stories progressed, the brothel became a place of darkness and evil. It eventually needed to come to its end and Sam was the man to do it.

Algonquin to English Translations

Bczon nikanaki – General greeting
Elakómkwik – Family
Gitche Manitou – Great spirit
Hakiwisilaasamamo Waswasimamo? – How are you?
Ke'eeps – Chicken or coward
Kitchi – Brave
Kuwumáras – I love you
Kwey – Algonquin greeting
Meegwetch – Thank you
Miigwech – Thank you
Moinguena – Shit-face
Munumayenok – Husband
Neia – Thanks
Nitáp – My friend
Niwisilasimamo – General reply
Nomattimen – Brother
Nunaumonittumwos – Wife
Otshee Monetoo – Evil spirit
Pígsuck – Pig dog
Qunnuhquitugk – Tall tree
Saskehavas – Bigfoot or Mountain People
Theemetha – Brother
Tic-kee! – Don't!
Wequanunk – Tree stump
Wematin – Brotherhood
Wetompasin – Female friend/sister
Wha-she-sho-wee-ko – Foolish white man

Native American Monsters & Demons

Hestovatohkeo'o – In some tribes Two-Faces are described as ogres, but most often the Two-Face resembles a human except for having a second face on the back side of his or her head. If people make eye contact with this second face, they will either be struck dead or paralyzed with fear until the Two-Face returns to murder them.

Mishipeshu – translates into "the Great Lynx". It has the head and paws of a giant cat but is covered in scales and has dagger-like spikes running along its back and tail.

Gitche Manitou – means Great Spirit, the Creator of all things and the Giver of Life, and is sometimes translated as the "Great Mystery".

Otshee Monetoo – It is omnipresent and manifests everywhere: organisms, the environment, events, etc. Aashaa Monetoo means "good spirit," while Otshee Monetoo means "bad spirit".

Tah-tah-kle'-ah – Giant owl witches who once roamed the plains at night looking for people to devour. They most enjoyed feasting on children and could mimic the languages of the tribes to lure victims.

Pukwudgie – are magical little people of the forest in Algonquian folklore, similar to European gnomes or fairies. Pukwudgie stories are told throughout the northeastern United States, southeastern Canada, and the Great Lakes region.

Windigo – a cannibalistic monster that preys on the weak and socially disconnected. In most versions of the legend, a human becomes a windigo after his or her spirit is corrupted by greed or weakened by extreme conditions, such as hunger and cold.

Saskehavas – or Sasquatch, according to Halkomelem and other Coast Salish traditions, Saskehavas were a powerful but generally benign supernatural creature in the shape of a very large, hairy wild man.

Mark Masztal is an award-winning illustrator and designer. He is known in the comic book field as the artist and co-creator of the Shar-Pei series, recently collected as the *Chronicles of Shar-Pei*.

Along with Michael Dobbs, Mark is the co-founder of Bing Comic Con, a 1-day pop culture event in Springfield, MA.

He spends his spare time volunteering for and representing Greyhound Options as their Vice President.

He was born and raised in Massachusetts, where he lives with his understanding wife Kathy and his dog, Cady.

This is his first short story collection. If you enjoyed the adventures of Resurrection Sam, don't worry, Sam will return in *Decades*, in 2023.

He can be found at www.masztal.com, and on Facebook and Instagram.

"Resurrection means that the worst thing is never the last thing."

- Frederick Buechner.

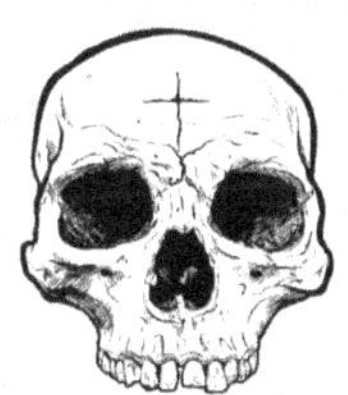